Savvy Girl

Savvy Girl

Lynn Messina

Harcourt, Inc.

Orlando   Austin   New York   San Diego   London

www.HarcourtBooks.com

Library of Congress Cataloging-in-Publication Data
Messina, Lynn (Lynn Ann), 1972–
Savvy Girl/Lynn Messina.
p.   cm.
Summary: A high school student gets a summer internship at a women's magazine
and a chance to write her own column, but is sidetracked by a new friendship
with a glamorous fashion editor.
[1. Internship programs—Fiction.   2. Journalism—Fiction.   3. Publishers and
publishing—Fiction.   4. Coming of age—Fiction.]   I. Title.
PZ7.M556Sav   2008
[Fic]—dc22   2007025671
ISBN 978-0-15-206161-6

Text set in Adobe Caslon
Designed by Cathy Riggs

First edition
A C E G H F D B

Printed in the United States of America

For Mom

Savvy Girl

Coordinate Your Outfit with Your Office:

EASY TIPS FOR FITTING IN

They announce the Savvy Girl competition on our very first morning.

We're barely two hours into our eight-week stint as interns at *Savvy* magazine when Georgie Brungart, the editor in chief, explains that in honor of the magazine's twenty-fifth anniversary, she's adding a new page called Savvy Girl and it's to be written by, yes, a Savvy Girl.

This statement sets off a murmur of excitement in the conference room. The entire staff of *Savvy* has gathered for a breakfast welcoming the summer interns. This is not only my first company-sponsored meal but also my first corporate meeting, and so far everything is going according to plan. I expect croissants and sliced melon and murmur-inducing statements from the editor in chief. I spent weeks fantasizing about what my first day at *Savvy* would be like

1

and am hugely relieved that it's already all that I've imagined. (Who says television doesn't represent life realistically?)

The girl next to me passes the fruit tray, and I take three slices of cantaloupe. I'd much rather have a croissant, but I'm afraid of leaving a crummy mess. I want to make a great impression.

So far I'm not doing a very good job. My outfit—a gray pinstripe skirt to my knees topped with a white collared shirt—isn't the height of corporate-casual chic I imagined it was when I was getting dressed this morning. Far from looking professional and glamorous, I look dowdy and boring. Everyone else is wearing bright colors like they've just stepped out of a *Savvy* layout—June's spread on New York summer style, to be precise ("Purse Overboard: Shed your hefty winter satchel in favor of a whimsical wristlet. Your shoulder will thank you"). Even my three fellow interns got the memo. The girl across from me is wearing a silver cami and hot pink skirt. The intern to her right is sporting almost the exact same thing, except her top is cotton and her micromini is sky blue.

I feel like such a dork.

When the room is quiet again, Georgie continues. "As many of you know, high school seniors now rank *Savvy* as their favorite magazine, ahead of *Allure* and *Glamour*. We want to develop that readership, to nourish and watch it grow as we ourselves grow. With a little effort and the help of each and every one of you, I know that one day very soon

Savvy will be the most widely read women's magazine in the United States. You know we can do it. To that end—"

Georgie pauses when the cheering becomes too loud. Everyone is thrilled by the idea of *Savvy*'s superstellar success and we can't help clapping excitedly, even me, who has worked here for less than two hours. A few editors hoot and the dark-haired girl next to me says "You bet" as she fist-pumps the air. It's like being at a high school pep rally but different because we're rallying around something real and important, not a crappy football team that always finishes second to last.

"To that end," Georgie says over the lingering noise, "we're going to have a high school student write the column. She'll be a senior, college-bound and very smart. She'll address the issues of the day but from a seventeen-year-old's point of view, adding a fresh perspective to the magazine and giving readers the straight dope."

Hearing "straight dope," I cringe. Georgie has been using slang like that all morning without any irony. She seems to think it's okay for forty-something editors in high-rise Manhattan office buildings to try to talk like teenagers. It's supposed to make her look with it, but all it does is make her look silly. If I were to write the Savvy Girl page, my first column would be about older people trying to sound young and vice versa. My advice: Act your age. (Unless your age happens to be too young to drink. In that case, act twenty-one.)

"The search for the Savvy Girl begins right now," she says. The tray of melon and strawberries lands in front of her and she selects a few pieces as she talks. "This year, we've assembled a talented assortment of interns from high schools across the country. Each of these aspiring young journalists, whom you've just met today—Lara, Hallie, Beth, and Chrissy—has what it takes to be the Savvy Girl, but only one will get the honor. The question that remains is which one. So, ladies," she says, looking at each of us in turn, "are you up for the challenge?"

I'm so shocked I don't know what to say. The idea of my very own page in my most favorite magazine ever is so exciting, so incredibly exhilarating, I can barely form a complete thought, let alone a whole sentence. The possibilities are staggering. It's . . . It's . . . It's everything I've ever wanted. Seriously: a dream come true. And not simply because having my own national column at the age of seventeen would be beyond prestigious. No, as much as I'd love the fame (imagine: girls in faraway places like Des Moines, Iowa, and Eugene, Oregon, knowing my name) and admiration (admissions officers at Columbia would have to let me in, right?), the straight-dope reason I want to be the Savvy Girl is I have something important to contribute. I've spent years carefully observing my peers and the culture at large and know for a fact that I can add to the national debate. I am a point of light. And if my fellow students at Roosevelt High look at me a little differently, perhaps with respect in their eyes, well, that's just icing.

My heart racing wildly, I take several deep breaths to calm down. It's too soon to get excited or to envision the sort of letters my readers will send ("Dear Chrissy: Thank you for your insightful article on race relations. It has changed my life"). First I have to get it. The selection process will probably be as long and complicated as the application for the internship itself. I had to beat thirty-two hundred candidates, fill out seven forms, get four recommendations, write three essays, and survive one tribunal with every senior editor at *Savvy* hammering questions at me like Supreme Court judges on speed.

As if reading my thoughts, Georgie raises her hand to silence the chatter and says, "The selection process will be simple and straightforward. All we need from each candidate is a thousand-word writing sample in the style you think most appropriate. You are, in effect, writing your first column. I, along with Lisa and Donna"—executive editor and features director, respectively—"will read the entries and decide who will write the Savvy Girl page for a full year, starting with January's special twenty-fifth-anniversary issue. The Savvy Girl will get a ten-thousand-dollar scholarship toward the school of her choice. Stories are due Friday, August twenty-third, one week before your internship ends, to give you the opportunity to incorporate as much as you learn here as possible. We will announce the winner at the good-bye breakfast for the interns on their last day."

August 23rd is seven weeks away, which gives me plenty of time to write the perfect Savvy Girl article. The hard part will be finding the right theme. My topic will have to be extremely relevant, something that really speaks to the young women of today. Maybe even controversial, like abortion. That's certainly relevant to my generation. I jot down the idea in my notebook to keep on the back burner. It's a good start.

"If you have any questions, please feel free to ask Lisa. She has all the details," Georgie says, taking off her retro glasses (vintage sixties, cat's-eye frames—so cool) and folding them in front of her.

The meeting breaks up a few minutes later, and as people file out of the room, I wrap two croissants in a napkin for lunch. As interns, we get only ten dollars a day to cover food and travel costs, which doesn't really cover anything. The train from Long Island alone runs four dollars per trip.

While I'm walking back to my desk, I hear someone call, "Hey, Chrissy." I turn around to see Hallie a few steps behind. She's the intern in the beauty department (I'm in health) and sits one cube closer to the window than me. I have a sliver of sky while she has an honest-to-god chunk. Not that I'm here for the view, of course.

"Isn't this the best thing ever?" she asks, her eyes sparkling with excitement. Hallie's very pretty, with shoulder-length brown hair that flips up at the end and freckles across her nose. Her frame is tiny; she barely reaches my shoulder, so I feel huge walking next to her, which is insane. I'm only five-foot-five. Not exactly a giant.

"It's a great opportunity," I agree.

Hallie also took a doggie bag from the meeting but she went with the healthy option of melon and strawberries. She stops in the kitchen to grab a bottle of Evian from the fridge. I didn't know there was water in the fridge, let alone that we are allowed to take it (um, I didn't even know there was a fridge). "Any ideas what you're gonna write about?"

Although I have thoughts, I'm not naïve enough to share them. Savvy Girl *is* a cutthroat competition like *American Idol.* The editors might as well have America call in to vote on who they like best. "No. I'll have to think about it for a while. You?"

She shrugs. "I don't want to zoom in on something too soon but I have a pretty good idea of what I want to do."

I nod casually like I'm not intimidated by her decisiveness. "That's cool. You can get started right away."

"I know. I think I'll do some tonight," she says.

At the end of the hallway, I pause to figure out which direction to go but Hallie turns to the right without even looking. Wow. She has a Savvy Girl topic *and* knows her way around. It's so annoying.

As we walk to our cubes, I take a good look around. Clutter, I see right away, is vital for making the right impression. All the editors have piles and piles of paper on their desk and colorful sticky notes posted everywhere. My workstation is disturbingly bare. I don't have anything but a Webster's word-a-day calendar and a framed snapshot. If I want to fit in, I'll have to start acquiring clutter immediately.

When I get back to my desk, I put the croissant-filled

napkin and free Evian in a drawer and reach for a manila folder. I write "Word, Daily" on the label, then tear off July 5th ("Pyrrhic: achieved at excessive cost <a *Pyrrhic* victory>"), even though the day isn't done. I stick it in the folder, which I place in a metal stand on my desk. I lean back in my chair, swivel back and forth a few times to get a one-eighty view, and decide it's a strong start. Next I create a file called Memos and print out everything that's been sent to my e-mail account at Mulhville-Moore Publishing, *Savvy*'s parent company. It's not much but it's important stuff like hiring announcements (a new VP of marketing!) and changes to the 401(k) plan. Two folders look twice as good as one. My in-box is pathetically low, so I add a stack of blank photocopy paper to fill it out and put the staff phone list on top.

I stand back and admire my handiwork. My desk has more stuff on it but it's far from the disorganized mess I'm hoping for. For real clutter, I need Post-it notes and unopened envelopes. To compensate (because I can't really address letters to myself and send them off), I concentrate on the shelves, which are still bare. All I have are a dictionary and the employee handbook. I stare at them for a bit, wondering how to fix things; then inspiration strikes. Duh. I work at a magazine.

I pick up twelve recent issues of *Savvy* from the closet outside Georgie's office and put them on the top shelf.

There, I think, eyeing my handiwork, *perfect.* Now I can

start writing deeply meaningful articles about the important health issues facing young women today. All I need is an assignment.

"Looks good," says Hallie admiringly. She's standing over my shoulder, watching.

A hot blush covers my cheeks. It's so embarrassing to be caught beefing up your workspace.

I shrug like I'm not completely flustered, and Hallie takes this as a cue to come visit. Her desk is as bare as mine used to be, but she has a copy of the *New York Times* next to her computer. Nice touch.

Hallie picks up my calendar. If she happens to notice that it's one day ahead, she doesn't comment on it. "This is neat," she observes. "I used to have one just like it in junior high. My grandmother got it for me for Christmas."

Next she picks up the snapshot, which is of me with a wax sculpture of the Dalai Lama at Madame Tussaud's (the one in Times Square, not even London, because it's not like I've actually ever left the country; Canada so doesn't count). It's not the best photo I've ever taken but it's one of my dad's favorites. He handed it to me this morning as we stepped outside Penn Station. He said, "You forgot your good luck charm." Harmless enough words but you should have seen the pride in his eyes: he and his little girl commuting together. Like it was something he'd dreamed of from the moment the nurse handed me to him in the maternity ward.

"Oh, the Dalai. Isn't he fabulous?" Hallie says in a mushy, gushy tone. "I saw him at Rutgers in Jersey. Had my mind totally blown. Didn't you?"

I open my mouth to explain that it's just a wax statue but she doesn't give me a chance. "How long did you have to wait to meet him? I waited two hours but it was so worth it. Look at him. Doesn't he just exude wisdom?" She sighs. Then wrinkles her nose. "He doesn't look right."

"What?" How can she tell? You can barely see the Sting statue's left hand in the background.

"When you saw him speak, was he sick or something? He looks all waxy here."

It's the perfect time to jump in with: *Funny you should mention wax.* But I can't do it. In a blinding flash, I can see it clearly—how pathetically juvenile it is not only to take your photo with a fake celebrity but to go to Madame Tussaud's at all (even the one in London). It's so younger-sister-in-junior-high, and I know Hallie will say so.

"You think so?" I say, grabbing the photo out of her hand. I examine it closely for evidence of fraud, but he still seems real enough to me. Bald head, kindly smile, saffron robe—there's nothing here to raise suspicion. Unless one has extrasensory perception. "That's weird. He was in top form that day. Look at that furrowed brow. I think he'd just said something insightful about the oppressiveness of the Chinese government. I'm pretty sure the woman behind me in line started crying. Anyway, this is some intern program, huh? I loved the breakfast we got this morning. The croissants looked delish. Did you try one?"

It seems like a reasonable question, even if the topic change isn't the smoothest one in the world (um, can you say free association?), but she doesn't fall for it. She narrows her eyes. My heart drops.

"It's fake, isn't it?" she asks, her tone gleeful—and loud. It's amazing how far sound travels in the large office. An editor two rows over raises her head. I lower mine. "It's, like, you and a cardboard cutout or something."

I nod. "He's wax," I admit. She's seeking confirmation and I give it. I don't know why. Everyone knows what you're supposed to do: Deny, deny, deny.

"Gosh, that's so cute. You take pictures with wax statues and then pass them off as real people. Does anyone fall for it? Here, let's see," she says, her tone amused, not vicious, as she stops the first person to walk by: the health editor, Lois McQuilken, aka my new boss.

I want the earth to swallow me up where I stand.

"Lois, have you seen this photo of Chrissy and the Dalai Lama?" Hallie asks easily, not at all self-conscious about wasting an important senior editor's time with the most trivial matter in the world. I'm amazed at her nerve.

Although Lois is clearly in the middle of something important (she's holding a ton of layouts—can Hallie not see that?), she doesn't seem to mind stopping. "The Dalai Lama?" she asks, leaning in to look at the photo.

"Yes, the Dalai Lama," Hallie replies, winking at me as if I'm in on the joke. Like: We're both putting one over on the unsuspecting editor.

The moment is excruciating. I don't know what I expected to happen—it seems unlikely that an important *Savvy* editor would care one way or another about my snapshot—but I feel a sense of impending doom. The world is about to end.

But I'm entirely wrong. The world doesn't end; the humiliation goes on and on.

"Good shot," Lois says with a smile. "We've got some great new Retin-A products if you get breakouts like that a lot."

Breakout? What breakout? My skin had been perfectly clear that day (otherwise: no photos). Okay, so maybe there was one little pimple on my forehead. But it was tiny. Like a pinprick. She couldn't possibly see that, could she? And if so, does that really constitute a breakout? And what about now? I have a million blackheads on my chin. I can't help it. I was so stressed about starting the internship that new ones keep popping up daily no matter how much zit cream I apply.

"I think we have some in the beauty closet," Lois continues, entirely unaware that her casual observation has sent me into a tailspin. "I'll take a look later."

"Thank you. I'd appreciate that," I say, amazed at how calm I sound. I thought for sure my voice would be sad and pathetic. Like the pip-squeaky little bleep of a mouse.

"No problem. One of the perks of the job is getting to

raid the beauty closet. Remind me to show it to you later," Lois says before walking away. Seconds later, she disappears inside the executive editor's office.

Delighted with the experiment, Hallie shows the photo to everyone in a three-cube radius. She starts with our fellow high school interns. Lara, assigned to the entertainment editor, giggles and asks me who else I've "met." Beth, who's in the articles department, is already too busy to make small talk. She simply rolls her eyes, which is an indictment all on its own. My cheeks burn.

Hallie then moves on to the low-level assistants around us. Most of them are too distracted by work to pay attention. They're all typing e-mails or about to pick up dry-cleaning or making lunch reservations, so the experience is slightly less humiliating. Not wanting to seem like a poor sport (I can totally laugh at myself), I try to ride it out with quiet dignity. I plaster a pleasant smile on my face while seething and imagining how humiliated Hallie will be when I win the Savvy Girl competition. (Someone should really be filming this. Why don't we have our own show on MTV?)

The whole thing seems almost bearable but then disaster strikes: The fashion editor, Jessica Cordero, drops by to find out which hotel her assistant booked the models into for the Jamaica shoot and notices us clustered around a neighboring desk. She peeks her head over and asks what's up.

Suddenly my knees go weak and I have to clutch the cube wall for support. The blood in my head starts pounding.

Of all the editors at *Savvy*, Jessica Cordero intimidates me the most. Blue-eyed and blond with a tiny, ski-jump nose, she's everything a fashion editor should be: tall, thin, beautiful, chic, British (her accent is faint, like Madonna's, but totally genuine). Her life is one glamorous event after another—runway shows, photo shoots, opening parties— and her personal wardrobe is augmented by the miles of clothing in the fashion closet. Free travel, free clothes, free food—her life is perfect.

Usually I'm not a fashion groupie. I like clothes but I don't obsess over them like some people. They serve a practical function: to make me look good (sometimes better than others). But Jessica Cordero is more than a fashion editor. She's a role model, an icon, an example of everything I want to be when I grow up.

Her life story is simple but storybook: At fourteen she was discovered by the fashion director of British *Vogue* while shopping with her friends at a flea market. At fifteen she appeared in runway shows for all the top designers in Milan, Paris, London, and New York. At eighteen, she quit modeling to go to college. She wanted to live a normal life: to hang out with friends, eat hot fudge sundaes, obsess about boys, and feel better about her body. She graduated Cambridge at the top of her class, moved to Manhattan, got a job as a lowly assistant editor at *Savvy*, and in three years worked her way up to become the youngest fashion editor in New York City.

She could have been the next Heidi Klum. Victoria's

Secret had offered her a million-dollar contract, but she turned it down to pursue something meaningful and real. In one of those character-defining moments when you find out who you really are, she chose substance over style. And that's who I want to be: the person who makes the right decision at crunch time. That's glamour.

Hallie isn't in awe of Jessica and shows her the photo without hesitating. *Hallie's* knees aren't weak. "It's fake," she explains, "but Chrissy likes to pass it off as real. Isn't that adorable?"

The way she says *adorable*—with calculated slowness, emphasizing each syllable in its turn: "a-dor-a-ble"— makes the situation too painful to bear. Even quiet dignity has its limits.

I turn abruptly and walk away, breezing past my desk. I need to get away—far, far away—from Hallie's mocking voice. But where to go? The cafeteria? No, it closed ten minutes ago. The stairwell? Too open. Someone might see. The bathroom? Bingo.

But picking a place to go is one thing; finding it is another. I have no idea where anything is (least of all my desk) and I circle the floor three times before somehow stumbling across the right hallway.

By the time I lock myself in a stall, I'm on the verge of tears. I don't know why I'm so upset. It's only a stupid photo. Nobody cares. Jessica Cordero definitely doesn't. She has better things to worry about (models, hotels, Jamaica) than a picture of a nameless intern with the Dalai

Lama, real or otherwise. Only Hallie cares, and her interest in the photo reveals more about her than me. In making me look silly she made herself look sillier.

Nevertheless, my heart is racing a million beats per second and my throat is curiously full. Any second now, I'm going to start crying. It's so pathetic. Only hours into my career and already I'm behaving like a scared little girl. What kind of journalist does that make me?

The weepy kind, I think mockingly. My editors will send me to cover heartwarming stories like "Panda Gives Birth in Captivity" or "Dog Saved from Burning Building by One-Armed Firefighter." I might as well give up now and become a greeting-card writer.

It's too terrible to think about, and I try to pull myself together. I'm made of sterner stuff than this. I have to be. I'm going to be an internationally renowned reporter, and internationally renowned reporters don't cry. They don't have any emotions. So I won't, either.

But even as I resolve to be strong and heartless, the tears start falling.

OFFICE SURVIVAL GUIDE:

DOS AND DON'TS
FOR IMPRESSING YOUR
COLLEAGUES

The next morning Adele Stuber gives me the rundown of the health department. It's made up of three people (not counting me, of course): Lois, senior editor; Adele, associate editor; and Holly, editorial assistant. Every month the department is responsible for eighteen pages. These include "Stat!," a page with flashy headlines about recent developments in the health field, anything from a just-published study on cholesterol to new diet products; "Diet 411," a mix of eating and exercise tips from celebrities; "The Big Q," a Q and A with a trained medical professional; "Chef's Table," nutritious, low-cal recipes from famous restaurants around the country; "Fit 1 2 3," an easy-to-follow exercise routine with step-by-step illustrations and an insightful article about an important health issue.

Savvy is a great mix of health stories, celebrity news,

relationship (read: *sex*) advice, fashion spreads, beauty info, and career tips. In a lot of ways, it's like *Cosmopolitan* or *Glamour,* but its vibe is more down to earth. *Savvy's* DIY tone makes you feel good about yourself, as if anything is possible. Even the monthly sex feature, "The Story of Oh, Yes," offers practical advice as opposed to other magazines' articles, which can make you feel like you have to be a cross between a trapeze artist and a gynecologist to do anything right (but don't get me wrong: I *love Cosmo*).

I think this is why *Savvy* appeals so strongly to girls my age. We need something mature to read—god forbid you get caught reading *Seventeen* when you're actually seventeen (or sixteen, or, let's be honest, fifteen)—that isn't intimidating.

"In the health department," Adele says as she opens an Excel spreadsheet, "our governing philosophy is that we're cheerleaders rooting our readers across the finish line. Remember, success is always within easy reach. The section has lots of elements that have to come together each month. We never get everything all at once so we have to keep track of each little piece. And by we, I mean you." She tilts the computer toward me so I can see the screen more clearly. "This is our trafficking document. Here's where you enter each story as it comes in and then track its progress through the system. It's going to be your responsibility to keep it up to date."

I nod and take notes as she defines the abbreviations. There's a lot of information and she throws it at me quickly, but I don't want her to think I can't keep up so I let some things slide. I can always ask questions later.

As Adele explains the system, it becomes glaringly obvious that a major consumer magazine is a lot more complicated than a high school newspaper. As the editor of Franklin D. Roosevelt High's *Roosevelt Report*, I'm in charge of coordinating all the little elements, but each monthly issue has only four spreads. It's less than half the size of *Savvy*'s health section. I can coordinate those elements during my lunch period.

Adele closes the Excel document and hands me a folder filled with press releases. "These are for the Stat! page. Read through them and set aside any that seem interesting. Lois likes dieting stories," she says, which, as a reader, doesn't surprise me. Weight loss is a huge focus of the magazine. Every month there's at least one major article on how to drop pounds effectively—and it's always upbeat and encouraging, like losing weight is something anyone can do. In *Savvy* they believe dieting should be painless, and specialize in diets that aren't really diets and exercise routines that don't require much movement. Everything they write is tailored to fit the modern woman's busy lifestyle, and I often find myself inspired by the stories. Sometimes I can hardly wait to graduate college and squeeze in Pilates between a meeting with my financial planner and cocktails with old high school friends.

"And these"—Adele puts a large box full of envelopes on her desk—"are query letters. We get a ton of them a week so there's always a backlog. Whenever you have spare time, read a few letters. We're looking for original article ideas that are expressed well. Most of our stories are generated in house but we always make a point of reading the pitches. And by we, I mean you."

I nod each time she piles on a new responsibility and wait for her to get to the part where I write deeply meaningful articles about important health issues facing young women today. The reason the *Savvy* internship is so prestigious is high school students get to do important magazine work. It's not just photocopying, filing, faxing, and addressing like so many other programs.

But although my list of routine tasks is long, it doesn't include writing. When I have enough work to keep me busy for eight months (let alone eight weeks), Adele says that's all for the moment. "I'll let you know if anything else comes up."

I open my mouth to ask about reporting but Adele has already turned away. Before I can form a sentence, she's on the phone with her mother discussing floral arrangements.

I tell myself not to panic. Maybe it's too soon for reporting assignments. Maybe you have to prove yourself first. Or maybe Lois doles out that stuff.

This last thought sounds the most reasonable, and I return to my desk in a better state of mind—until I realize how much work I've got. There's so much, I have no idea where to start. I try to read the notes I've taken and realize they're mostly scribble. The only words I can make out are *press release,* so I begin there.

Across the aisle Adele's conversation switches from flowers to photographers. Because all the cubes are so close together, there's no privacy whatsoever and I hear every word of her conversation, as well as everyone else's in the surrounding area. Adele, however, is on the phone more than anybody. Her boyfriend of four years recently proposed and she's currently obsessed with planning the wedding. (He hid the ring in a bowl of wonton soup at the Szechuan Palace on Lexington and Twenty-eighth, "their" restaurant. She goes on about the proposal like it's the most romantic thing in the world—"the diamond dumpling," she calls it—but I think it's absolute cheese. When I get engaged, I'm totally saying no if the guy tries to choke me with the ring; I don't care how much I love him.)

As the week goes by I slowly realize that Adele has pawned off her entire job on me. She's too busy ordering favors and bullying her bridesmaids ("I don't care if your boobs fall out of the dress; you're not wearing the straps") to have time for even the most basic tasks. Although I like the responsibility and having important things to do, being busy every minute of the day is exhausting, and I arrive home every night at eight, thoroughly pooped. I eat dinner, veg out on the couch, and fall asleep around ten-thirty. I can't even make it till Jon Stewart. Since most of my friends have their own summer thing going on—being a counselor at a sleepaway camp or taking college prep courses or, in the case of Judy Klinger, traveling around Israel for six weeks with twenty-seven other teens from Long Island—it doesn't really matter that I'm comatose. There wouldn't be much to do even if I had the energy.

Much of the work is self-explanatory when I do it, but a couple of things are really confusing (um, I've never even seen an Excel spreadsheet before) and I have no idea what I'm doing. I've tried to ask Adele for help, but she's never available. Although she appears to spend most of her day sitting at her desk doing nothing, she's really on hold with the florist or printer or photographer, and the second you start to speak to her, the other person always comes on the line. It's so frustrating, sometimes I want to scream.

Lois isn't much better, but at least she is too busy with her job to answer my questions. She always tells me to check with Adele. Despite this, I think she's a good boss. She obviously knows the magazine business like the back of her hand and everyone comes to her for advice (that's why she's always in meetings). I don't see her much, which is disappointing because we never get to talk about my writing articles, but I think she's great. Every time she visits the beauty closet, she picks up something for me like wrinkle cream or antiaging serum. She's even promised to let me go in there with her on my last day and choose whatever I want. I can't wait. I'm going to snag pomade and shine spray and all those other pricey styling products Mom won't spring for.

When I absolutely, positively have no idea what I'm doing, I go to Holly, who only talks in monosyllables. The trick is figuring out the right questions to get useful answers. It's like playing with a Magic 8 Ball.

By Friday night I'm so done with *Savvy* I never want to go back. The excitement of being one of the chosen few has worn off. Now I feel like just another working stiff, and I wonder why I'm not at the beach with my best friend, Lily. Or counseling at a sleepaway camp in the Adirondacks like Helen. Or even at Princeton taking dead-boring classes on physics like Keely. Some days the sky is such an incredibly bright blue through my window crack that I feel a wave of sadness. This is my last summer before applying to college. I should be having fun.

The train pulls into Bellmore and I take the escalator down with a swarm of other commuters who, unlike my dad, aren't lucky enough to get half-day Fridays in the summer. I look for my mom's car but instead see the bright fire-engine red of Lily's Miata.

"Hey," I say, smiling widely. It's only been a week since I've seen her but it feels like forever. So much has happened. "What are you doing here?"

"I thought we could grab some takeout and eat it at the beach," she says, shades still on, even though the sun is about to drop below the horizon. "I know the patrol guys so they won't kick us out."

The beach Lily works at closes at dusk, but many of the local kids like to hang out after dark. It's pretty romantic and all with the sound of the crashing waves, the soft breeze, and the cool sand. Lily has made out on the beach more times than I can count, although I've only done it once. Jason Kilgrew. I thought I liked him but when he started kissing and touching me I realized I didn't, so we just sat on the blanket drinking beer and ignoring each other while everyone else had a good time. It's weird. You'd think I'd have figured it out before then but I really had no idea. I guess sometimes you have to get that close to someone to know.

"Sounds good." I get into the car and immediately lean forward to change the radio station. Lily has the worst taste in music. All disco. No rock. No hip-hop. No alt-country. Just cheesy driving beats that repeat over and over. It's like being trapped in a John Travolta flick.

She pulls out of the parking lot and I lean back, breathing in the warm summer air. Lily has the coolest car ever: a Mazda MX-5 Miata convertible. Her parents bought it from a cousin who was moving to Europe (Vienna or Venice or something); he'd barely taken it out of the garage. The car has less than five thousand miles on it and still smells brand-new. I'm stuck with the same crappy Ford Taurus (in beige: hello, middle age) that my sister, Jackie, dented the day after her road test and my brother, Roger, threw up in on his eighteenth birthday. The pickup's useless, the CD player scratches disks, and the windshield wipers have only one speed: superfast. So when it's drizzling out, I look like a nervous loser who's never driven a car before. It sucks.

Lily got the fabulous car through unfabulous circumstances: Her parents are getting divorced and are each trying to buy her loyalty. Her dad has been having an affair with his secretary for years, which her mom discovered when she made an unscheduled visit to his office after the Wednesday matinee of *Fiddler on the Roof.* She thought they could grab a quick lunch but Mr. Carmichael had already grabbed something (his secretary—so typical). The whole thing would have been devastating enough if the woman in question were half the age of Lily's mom, Vivienne, or a girl just out of her teens. But it turns out she's six years *older*. Which is really, really humiliating. Because if the dirty old man isn't in it for the nubile young flesh, then there must be something very wrong with his wife.

As soon as she returned from the city, Vivienne began throwing his stuff out the window (also typical). Lily got home just as she started tossing stereo equipment. After dodging Bose speakers she calmed her mom down somewhat, found out what happened, and suggested she talk to a marriage counselor. Vivienne went straight to the yellow pages to find the divorce lawyer with the largest ad.

Ever since Vivienne started divorce proceedings, she's been shopping like a madwoman. All Lily has to do is say she likes something for it to show up on her bed in a nicely wrapped package. In the last eight months her wardrobe has gone from whatever to wow. And Lily's clever. She knows how to play her parents against each other. The sad thing is she's only half playing. She's so hurt by her parents that her loyalty *is* for sale. Right now she's so angry at both at them she can't see beyond their checkbooks. (Hmm. Perhaps divorce and how it affects children would make a great Savvy Girl column. It's something to think about.)

Lily tries to blow off the whole broken-home thing like it's no big deal, but I know sometimes it's hard to handle. Her father, Jefferson Radley Carmichael the Third (Lily's so lucky she's not a boy), was never really around much, anyway—he's a pretty famous defense lawyer who's always getting guilty people off—but she liked the feeling of completeness that comes from being a family. I kinda know what she means. My brother, who's a congressional aide in DC, and my sister, a junior at Tufts, are rarely around, but when they are it's always nice to have a full set of Gibbonses at the dinner table, even if it means more dishes for me to wash. And my parents, for all their crappy-car-dom but happily-married-ness, are still pretty okay. They have the usual parental faults, like asking too many questions, but they know how to give a person space. Dad sells municipal bonds for Paine Webber and Mom answers phones for Glen Cove's most successful Realtor. Their jobs keep them busy.

We pick up cheeseburgers and french fries at Wendy's and drive to the beach, which is only ten minutes away. Lily leads me to her lifeguard station: a tall, wooden chair that she shares with a guy named Graham McPhee. He goes to some high school in Great Neck, one of those old-money Long Island towns with pricey boutiques on the main strip and large, pre-Levittown houses. He came out with us once, two weeks ago when we went into the city to see a band. Calypso Cataclysm does ironic, self-conscious punk rock. Lots of fun. Their music is good, but it's not *good*. Graham didn't get that. He kept talking about how fresh their sound was. Clearly, he was trying too hard. It got on my nerves, but Lily thought it was sweet and is seriously considering him for her new boyfriend. She's still sorta with the old one but that's how Lily operates. She chain-smokes guys.

"So?" she says as she leans back in the chair. Even in her retro prep-girl couture (high collar, pleated skirt, three shades of pastel), she looks like she belongs at the beach. It's not the bathing suit or whistle that makes her fit in; it's her blond hair, blue eyes, deep tan, and Miss America smile. Lily has always been the gorgeous one. Even smothered in calamine lotion with the chicken pox, she still had that teen-mag cover model perfection.

"So?" I repeat.

"How was the first week? Is it everything you thought it would be? Have you been assigned a cover story yet? What's your office like? Are the other interns nice? Details, details! I feel like I haven't talked to you in years."

This is true. I've been too tired at night to call her. After my first day at work I rang her from the train, but so many fellow commuters gave me dirty looks, I hung up after two sentences. I've never felt so judged in my entire life, which is saying a lot, especially having been through the *Savvy* inquisition.

I'm tempted to give her the same answer I give my parents ("It's great, thanks"), but she's my best friend, so I'm honest.

"Exhausting. Awful. Everybody's really mean," I say. It feels so good to spew. "No, that's not true. Only a few people are mean. One of the other interns, Hallie, won't stop teasing me about my fake Dalai Lama photo. She's evil. The associate editor, Adele, off-loaded her entire job on me so she can plan her wedding and doesn't even have the decency to tell me *how* to do her job. The editorial assistant, Holly, hates me because I do less photocopying than her and she doesn't seem to understand that she gets *paid* to do drone work. And the fashion editor gives me a look that says 'What are you doing here?' every single time she walks by me. The only person I like is my boss, Lois. She gave me some free acne cream from the beauty closet, which is just like we always imagined: a room packed to the gills with perfume, conditioner, shampoo, lotion, eye shadow. Everything you can think of. And the stuff she gave me is really expensive. I Googled. It costs like ninety dollars for four ounces."

"So you hate the internship?" she asks, staring out at the sea in the fading light. The line between ocean and sky is almost completely gone.

"No, it's fine. I just thought there'd be more writing. Oh, there's one supercool thing," I say, then explain about the Savvy Girl column.

Lily is as excited as I am. She knows how much this opportunity means to me. We've been friends for a really long time, since we were four years old. We met in nursery school. For weeks I came home every day saying "Lilky" until my mom finally called the teacher to ask if there was a Lilky in my class. The woman said, "No, but there's a Lily." My mom called her mom and set up a playdate and we've been hanging out ever since.

"Do you have any ideas?" she asks.

"I'm kicking around a few ideas, but nothing is solid yet," I say. The week was too crazy to think about topics. Coming up with a theme is the most important part of the competition, so I want to give it the concentration it deserves. It's not something you squeeze in between a telephone call and an Excel tutorial. (Unlike, say, planning the blowout party I'd throw if I won, which can totally be done on the fly: backyard barbecue; favorite foods like London broil, corn on the cob, and ice cream; invitations that say "Chrissy's Column Launch"; free copies of the issue.)

"What about you?" I ask after she tosses out a few ridiculous suggestions (how to get your parents to buy you an apartment in Soho, etc). "What's going on?"

"Same old. I ended things with Josh. He was getting really boring."

"Already?" I ask, although I'm not at all surprised. We

29

both knew it was coming. When you're Lily, all guys get boring after a while.

She shrugs. "He's got some office job in the city for the summer and it's all he can talk about. He thinks I'm interested in the people he works with."

"But you're interested in the people I work with," I point out.

"Yeah, but you're my best friend. I'm interested in your whole life," she says.

"So how's Graham?" I ask, knowing he's next up.

"He's great. Funny and sweet. You should give him another chance. If you got to know him better, I think you'd like him a lot."

Since he won't be around much longer than Josh or Nick or any of the others, it doesn't really matter if I like him or not. But I don't say that because my opinion obviously means something to her. "Okay. Maybe we'll all hang next week."

"Cool. Let's," she says with a smile. "So I wanna hear more about this evil hag Hallie. What can we do to get back at her? And don't say something juvenile like putting black ink in her Wite-Out. It's gotta be good."

I tell her revenge is not necessary or professional, but Lily pooh-poohs me and suggests we break into her Mulhville-Moore e-mail account and send dirty messages to the CEO. "With lots of four-letter words to really get things going."

It's a totally ridiculous idea (and talk about juvenile),

but we have fun sitting on the beach in the soft breeze composing letters. Lily's are graphic like Internet porn; mine are subtle, PG-13 masterpieces.

At ten we decide to get ice cream, and as we zip along the highway in Lily's little red car, I realize that for the first time in five days I'm finally relaxed. Even my dread of Monday has faded. I've got two whole days off with nothing to do. Hallelujah.

"Thank you," I say, grateful that she was at the station instead of my mom.

The wind is so loud, she doesn't hear me. I see her lips form the word *What?*

I say it again, shouting. She still doesn't understand and mouths *Huh?*

I shake my head and laugh. I don't have to thank her. Of course Lily was waiting for me when I got off the train at the end of the most grueling week of my life. That's what best friends do.

FATAL CRUSH
or
Hunger Pangs?

Take Our True Love Challenge

I fall in love with Michael Davies at the intern meet-and-greet, which is held on the Wednesday of our third week, even though one quarter of our internship has already passed and we're all pretty familiar with how things work at Mulhville-Moore. I see him before I talk to him and that's enough. He's absolutely gorgeous, with tousled black hair and a strong, chiseled jawline with a hint of stubble. Stubble! Nobody in my high school has that. And his eyes: They're the bluest blue in the whole entire world. Like a shade you see only on posters in travel agencies advertising idyllic tropical destinations. He knows how to pull off his look, too. In a tailored ice blue suit and black shirt, he looks like he just stepped off the pages of *GQ*. All the other guys are wearing some variation on boring old khakis. He's dressed to stand out.

The second I see him, my heart stops.

We're in a large conference room with a hundred other people so he doesn't notice me right away. A touchy-feely facilitator from human resources—she *so* thinks she's Oprah—is making us go around the room and introduce ourselves. You have to say four things: your name, what year of school you're in (*Savvy* is one of the few M-M publications that takes high school interns), your magazine, and what you hope to get out of the internship. I wait with bated breath for Mr. Gorgeous to go, impatiently listening to all the boring, not-gorgeous people before him. Nobody's answer to the fourth question is interesting. We all give polite, politically correct responses like "to get a better understanding of the publishing industry" and "to learn as much about magazines as possible."

When we get to Michael, I learn that he's a college junior at GW interning at *Egoïste,* a magazine like *Vanity Fair* but snarkier, and hopes to master the skills he needs for a career in publishing. It's the same old bullshit but he makes it sound meaningful.

After the introductions we take a food break. It's right around lunchtime but all they supply are desserts like brownies and cookies and Rice Krispies Treats. It's been hours since yogurt at breakfast, so I make a beeline for the Rice Krispies Treats, which I love. While other people are looking over the selection, I grab three and wrap them in a poufy wad of napkins so nobody can see how many I have. Then I debate snagging a fourth. I know I seem greedy, but

33

the next half of the meeting could be just as boring as the first and I need sugar. Someone from circulation is supposed to talk to us about the challenges of distribution. I think the real challenge of distribution is staying awake through a discussion of it.

By the time I decide I need one last treat to get me through the afternoon, they're all gone so I return to my chair. Next to me a girl is texting madly. Her thumbs fly across the touch pad with incredible dexterity and speed, and I watch—first discreetly out of the corner of my eye, then straight on when she doesn't notice—marveling at her absorption. Nothing around her, not even me staring like she's a sideshow freak, throws off her concentration. What could she possibly have to say that's so important? (Seriously: what?)

I'm so fascinated by her I don't notice a guy in the next row trying to get my attention. He brushes his fingers against my knee. Surprised, I jump out of my chair and squeal sharply. Not even this breaks her focus. Amazing.

"Hey," the guy says with a wave.

Oh, god. It's him.

I open my mouth to say something but I'm too stunned by the fact that his beautiful blue eyes are looking right into mine. Of course he's even more gorgeous up close. He eyelashes are thick, his nose straight, and his lips soft and pouty.

I feel very plain in comparison, even though I'm wearing a new outfit and my one pair of sexy shoes. I totally thought Mom would freak when she saw the stilettos ("Go back to your room, young lady, and blah blah blah"), but she simply laughed. And laughed. Suspicious, I asked her what was so funny. She shook her head, shrugged, and said "You'll see" in that annoying, Mother-knows-best tone I hate. (She was right, damn it. I'd barely stepped out of the front door before the shoes started killing me. My feet are throbbing terribly right now, which doesn't make any sense at all because I'm *not even standing*.)

Even though I don't have the best self-esteem in the world, I usually feel pretty okay about myself. I have long, curly brown hair with gold highlights and green eyes. I'm medium tall and medium thin. But Michael Davies's perfection is intimidating, and suddenly I feel painfully aware of all my flaws. My crooked nose. Like someone broke it in a bar fight. My thin lips that disappear when I smile. My high forehead. My wrestler's arms. My boringly average chest—not big enough to make boys drool, not flat enough to pull off couture knockoffs.

"Didn't mean to scare you," he says.

"You didn't," I say. I know I should add something funny and clever but all I'm capable of is flat denial.

"That's good," he says.

"Yeah," I agree.

A weird silence follows as I rack my brain, trying to come up with the perfect remark that will kick off a twenty-minute conversation and possibly a lifelong relationship.

"I couldn't help noticing you got yourself a nice little

stash of Rice Krispies Treats." He tilts his head downward and looks at my lap. My gaze follows his and suddenly I'm horrified. I'm holding three Rice Krispies Treats. Three. Like a big fat pig. *Oh, my god.* The heat of embarrassment hits my face with startling intensity. I don't think I've ever been so mortified in my whole life, and that's including the Dalai Lama incident.

"Oh, wow. These. Yeah. I don't. It's not . . ." Deep breath. Stay calm. "I know what it looks like, but actually I'm . . ." What? Think fast. I look around me, around the room, and notice the texting girl. "Getting for a bunch of people." Without thinking too much about it, I tap her on the shoulder. "Here you go. Your Rice Krispies Treat as promised."

The girl stares at me like I'm crazy. And no wonder. She has no idea who I am or even that I've been sitting next to her for the last hour, and now I'm forcing high-calorie confections on her. She opens her mouth to speak—probably to tell me to get lost.

"No need to thank me," I say in a rush. "It's my pleasure. Besides, I was going up there anyway."

The marshmallow square is still in my hand, hovering between my lap and hers, and all I can do is plead with her silently to take it. The girl looks at me, then at Michael, then at the Rice Krispies Treat. She's sizing up the situation. I can't imagine what this must seem like to her. A dare? A practical joke? A hazing ritual?

Nothing so nefarious, apparently, because she takes it from me. "Thanks," she says, "I've been looking forward to this all morning."

I'm so relieved, all I can do is smile.

"That's one down," Michael says. "Do I hear two?"

When I'm sure I can talk without stuttering, I turn back to him. "Two?"

"Yeah, does that second one have a name on it also? If it doesn't, I'd like to make a trade." He holds out a brownie and a chocolate chip cookie. "Take your pick."

"Oh, that's not necessary. You can have them," I say, offering both treats without thinking. It seems like the natural thing to do.

He smiles at me. He has a killer smile: perfect teeth, dimples. "Hey, that's great. You're so cool." While I'm replaying the compliment in my head and gloating, he reaches for the wad of napkins with the two treats. "I appreciate this. Are you sure you don't want something? Here, have the brownie. It has nuts."

Although I don't like nuts in baked goods—in nut bowls, yes—I take it, admiring his sense of fair play. He didn't have to give me anything. Clearly he's a man of strong principle.

I thank him and then struggle to come up with more conversation. If I don't ask him something now, he might leave my life forever. "So you're at *Egoïste*?"

"Hey, great memory."

Two compliments in two minutes—not bad considering my slow start. "How is it?"

He shrugs. "All right. A lot of famous writers come through who think they're the shit, so that gets old really quick."

I can't imagine anything more exciting than working with real-life *New York Times* bestsellers (except maybe *being* a *NYT* bestseller), but I suppose I know where he's coming from. With people that big, there are probably a lot of egos involved. "I'm at *Savvy*," I volunteer. When he doesn't comment, I add, "We don't have a lot of famous writers but many of our editors are pretty self-involved." I'm thinking, of course, of Adele. Even though I've managed to do everything she's asked during the last two weeks—and in a prompt and efficient manner that often has me working through lunch—she's never given me a single compliment. Not one "Good job, Gibbons."

Michael nods but before he can say anything, the Oprah wannabe announces that our speaker is ready to start. He stands up to return to the other side of the room. "Thanks again," he says.

Transfixed, I watch him walk past the podium and sit down. He eats one Rice Krispies Treat immediately and puts the other away for later. That's *exactly* what I would have done. Wow. We have so much in common.

The circulation VP is thirty-something and slick. He's big on eye contact and winking, and he keeps asking rhetorical questions that some people (like Hallie) raise their hands to answer. He does his best to make his talk interesting but it's impossible; the topic is a total snooze.

Next to me, the texting girl continues to tap out messages. She never once looks up but at one point she glances at the brownie out of the corner of her eye and says, "Are you gonna eat that?"

I sigh and hand it over.

YOU *GLOW,* GIRL!

'm looking forward to Mulhville-Moore's big sixty-eighth anniversary bash at the Four Seasons Hotel for two reasons. One: I've never been to a glitzy publishing party before. Two: Michael Davies will be there. It's been two whole weeks since we met, and although I hang out every morning in the lobby, I've only bumped into him once. It's so not fair. I stay down there as long as possible, pretending to be so engrossed in the *Times* that I don't even notice the elevator coming and going. But I can pull this off only for about ten minutes before I start to worry about the security guards getting suspicious. I'd totally die if they thought I was a terrorist or something.

To fix this problem, I keep moving around my arrival time, which has my father, who has taken the same 8:12 A.M.

commuter train for twenty-two years, confused. First I came a full half-hour early, at 9:30. When that didn't work, I switched it to a full half-hour late, 10:30. Neither made a difference. The one time our paths did cross, I almost missed him because I was deeply engrossed in a memo that Lois had had me type up (such irony!). He was getting on the elevator as I was walking by, and all I got to do was wave and say hey before the doors closed on his beautiful face. I'm still not sure if he knew who I was.

Because I don't want a repeat of day one, I spent most of the weekend shopping for an outfit for the party. It's not like me to stress so much about clothes, but being around the editors at *Savvy,* who always look perfect, makes me feel self-conscious. Even the other interns look at if they have personal stylists putting together their outfits each morning. The whole building is like that. Every day I ride up in the elevator with women who have a highly developed fashion sense.

The thought of going to a big-deal event with them is intimidating, which is why I dragged Lily to her favorite boutique in Nolita on Saturday. While trying on different tops, skirts, and dresses, I considered using the experience for my Savvy Girl article. It's hard to have confidence in yourself when you feel like an ugly duckling in the shadow of swans. It's a superficial thing and I'm smart enough to know better, but the feeling is hard to shake. Appearance sometimes is reality.

When I arrived this morning, I was happy with my selection and felt very swanlike. Now, as editors dart past my desk in evening gowns, my confidence starts to wither and fade. My outfit is once again all wrong. I look way too casual, like I'm going to a Long Island dance club on a Friday night. The top is bronze, with embroidered pink flowers and red rhinestones; the skirt is black and silky and really short. Although it struck me as a little *too* short, Lily insisted I buy it. She said the trashy look might have gone out with Britney but guys still go for it.

Guys maybe, but probably not the doorman at the Four Seasons.

Adele walks by in a floor-length black dress, and I order myself to remain calm. It's not the end of the world.

Still, I look at my watch—5:15—and calculate that there's just enough time to run across to the street to the Gap and pick up something unsparkly and tasteful. But how would I pay for it? I only have twenty dollars in my wallet, and I blew my entire allowance on this outfit.

There's always my emergency credit card, which is supposed to be used in only the most desperate situations. I am pretty sure this qualifies—there's nothing more desperate than being tossed out of the Four Seasons on your silky black butt with all your coworkers and your soul mate watching—but I'm not sure my parents would agree. They're very fussy about what makes up an "emergency" and seem to consider only those situations that entail potential bodily harm. Perhaps I could mention the bruises I'd get when they kick me to the curb for looking like a stripper in a sex shop. Then perhaps they'd be cool with it.

No, I'd better not. That would open a whole other can of worms.

What to do?

"Hey, great top," a voice says.

I look up. It's Jessica Cordero, fashion editor and most amazing person ever. Standing next to my desk. Complimenting me. I open up my mouth to thank her but I'm too stunned to say anything but "really" in a completely amazed tone. Like: "*Real*-ly?" So not cool. She probably thinks I've never gotten a compliment before.

She nods. I can't believe it. *The* Jessica Cordero standing next to my desk, nodding at me. "Yeah," she says. "It's fabulous. We just shot something similar for the December issue. Very deck-the-halls."

Shot something similar? Now I'm finding it even harder to form a sentence. I stutter thank you, my eyes so wide from shock I must look like an owl.

Jessica doesn't seem to notice. She rests her hip against my desk and folds her arms across her chest. I stare up at her, wondering if I should stand or something. Maybe offer her a cup of coffee. But I don't have coffee or even a stick of gum. I'm a terrible hostess.

"Where'd you get it?" she asks, obviously unaware of how much her attention is freaking me out.

For a moment I blank. There's nothing in my head except the image of a little red Tic Tac that might be on the bottom of my purse. But I can't offer her that. Focus. Where'd I get the top? Wait. I know this one. Red Bars? Red Jars? "Red Mars," I blurt out.

Jessica picks up a snow globe of the famous Petronas Towers in Kuala Lumpur. I snagged it from the giveaway table, where editors leave promotional items they don't want. Mostly it's doodads and snacks but sometimes really great things show up, like sneakers or earrings. You have to move fast, though. Everyone keeps an eye on the giveaway table, especially Carmen O'Brien, the copy chief, whose office is directly across from it. She has a stable of freelance copy editors (they do all the term-paper stuff, like making sure words are spelled correctly and commas are in the right places) and is always grabbing the best things for them. She even keeps a file with all their sizes: shoe, waist, bra. It's amazing.

"On Mulberry, right?" Jessica says, shaking the globe from the Malaysian tourist board. Glitter swirls around the towers.

I can't say for certain which street it's on because I usually just follow Lily from the subway, but I agree with her anyway. "Yeah."

She nods approvingly—at me. Wow. "I get tons of stuff there. I'm impressed, Gibbons. You've got great taste."

It's one of the best compliments I've ever been given— she a *fashion* editor and former *model*—and I'm still basking in it when Adele walks by. She notices I've hardly made a dent in the stack of magazines she wants me to send out and gives me a stern look. It's supposed to propel me into action but I ignore it. I know I should care that she's annoyed with me, but I don't. I can't. The coolest person on the face of the earth is leaning her hip against my desk. I have much more important things to think about. Such as asking Jessica how hard it was to give up modeling and what she studied at Cambridge and why she came to New York instead of London or Paris or Milan. I want to *know* her. The info I've managed to glean from Google is just gossip. Even the profile *Egoïste* ran years ago when she was at the top of the fashion world was mostly gushing hearsay.

Jessica watches Adele walk down the hallway and shakes her head. "I'm always fascinated by my coworkers' choices," she says softly. "They think they're so chic and modish, but they've missed the point. Fashion is audacious, not safe and easy."

"You should see her wedding dress," I reply without thinking. The second the words are out of my mouth, I wish I could take them back. The bitchy comment is not my style, and I never like talking about people behind their backs; I'm too afraid of getting caught.

Still, I want to impress Jessica, and I can tell by her smile I've done it in the exact right way. Jessica smiles. "I don't have to. Tons of tulle, right? Lots of beaded pearls. A hoop skirt. Poufy sleeves. Lace gloves. Stop me if I'm wrong."

The dress isn't as bad as all that. It's tulle-heavy and beaded, but the sleeves are capped, not poufy. The bodice is actually pretty nice, with silk detailing and sleek lines.

But I know that's not what Jessica wants to hear. "No, you're on the money. Total Princess Di."

She rolls her eyes. "It's amazing how you can always call these things. Some people don't mind being a cliché. It's so tedious."

"Yeah," I say again.

Jessica checks out the scene as more and more editors desert their desks for the bathroom mirror. I also have to put on some makeup—glittery bronze shadow to match my top and lip gloss—but I don't want to move. If the fashion editor of *Savvy* doesn't realize she's chatting with a lowly high school intern, then I certainly don't want to be the one to point it out. She'll be taking off soon enough, I realize, looking at the time. It's already 5:40.

Apparently unaware of how late it is, Jessica slides onto my desk in one fluid motion. She puts down the snow globe and reaches for the photo of me with the wax Dalai Lama; she examines it closely. Outwardly, my expression doesn't change, even as the red heat rushes to my cheeks with uncomfortable intensity. Inwardly, however, I'm cringing with shame and chanting, *Damn it. Damn it. Damn it.* Of course I wanted to cut the photo into a million little pieces and stuff them into the toilet after Hallie mocked it. But even as I held the scissors in my hand, I couldn't do it. Getting rid of the picture would imply there's something wrong with it, and I have too much pride for that. So it sits on my desk between the telephone and the Webster's word-a-day calendar ("Hobson's choice: an

46

apparently free decision when there is no real alternative"), where any editor, including the coolest one at the magazine, can pick it up. Damn it.

"I have one of these," Jessica says after a moment.

"You do?" I ask, wide-eyed.

"Yeah, me and Ashton Kutcher and Ashton Kutcher. You know, dummy and real one side-by-side. Or, as my boyfriend at the time liked to say, 'dummy and dummy.' He was jealous. Ashton and I had a vibe."

My eyes—impossibly—open even wider. "You know Ashton Kutcher?"

"I did a photo shoot with him at Madame Tussaud's a few years back. The one in London. Not here. Only one of the models was a prima donna. Harley something or other. I'll never work with her again."

It's impossible not to be impressed: a former supermodel dissing the hottest supermodel of the moment.

Still, I don't want to *seem* so impressed. Only junior high school students gush. "Sounds like fun."

She smiles. "It was. I even went back a couple days later with my boyfriend, the jealous one. We broke up soon after. He was so possessive. Such a drag."

"I know how that can be," I say trying to sound wise, although I really have no idea. The only guy I've ever dated who showed even the remotest spark of jealousy was Matthew Zolat, and that was over his ex-girlfriend's date to the spring dance, a Hofstra sophomore with bulging biceps. I should have known something was up when he asked me out. The captain of the football team never hangs with the editor of the school paper. Being as smart as most jocks, he thought dating his ex's polar opposite would drive her crazy with jealousy, but it totally backfired. I felt really stupid after I figured out what was going on. Unfortunately, most of my dating experiences have been like that. Believe it or not, Matthew Zolat was one of my better relationships.

"Hey, you know, I should probably get going," Jessica says, putting down the photo next to the snow globe.

Even though I know she's got too much going on to chat with me all evening, I can't help feeling disappointed. It's been so cool to have her chill at my desk. But I smile brightly like it doesn't matter. "Yeah, it's getting late."

"Are you heading over there now?"

I peek at my watch and see that it's already a little after six. Darn it. I still have two dozen envelopes to stuff. I try to calculate how long it'll take to finish. "In a second," I answer vaguely.

"Cool. I'm ready to roll, too. Let's share a cab."

I look at the stack of magazines and weigh my options. I can do them now and be late or finish first thing in the morning before Adele arrives. It's not like I'm blowing off the job entirely. I mean, they can't go out tonight regardless. "Sounds good," I say as I open the top drawer of my desk and grab my purse. It's a little Coach number that Lily's mom bought her a few weeks ago. I'm the first one to use it.

Jessica slides off my desk. "Let me get my stuff. I'll meet you at the elevators in five?"

"It's a date."

Jessica walks away, and as soon as she's out of sight, I do a little happy dance in my chair. It's so exciting. I quickly survey the room to see if anyone noticed how much time she'd spent talking to me. Almost a full half hour. That's got to be a record. I've never seen her spend that much time in anyone else's cube, certainly not one of my fellow interns'. Unfortunately, nobody but Adele seems to have noticed her visit at all, let alone its lengthiness. They are all too busy curling their eyelashes and fluffing their hair and putting on earrings to pay any attention to me. Gosh, some people are *so* self-involved.

I drop into the bathroom for two minutes to apply makeup—only shadow and gloss because I don't want to keep Jessica waiting—then head to the reception area. She isn't there yet, but I press the down button so she won't have to wait long for an elevator. After two cars stop on the fortieth floor it seems for no reason, I reevaluate my strategy and decide to sit down on an overstuffed chair to wait for her. Recent issues of *Savvy* litter the table, and I pick up the June magazine, which I've read a million times before.

As I flip through the pages, I try to imagine where my Savvy Girl column will go. Maybe in the front, somewhere near the table of contents so even people who get bored with the issue will see it. Or perhaps on the very last page. Then if the back cover gets torn off, it'll be like I'm on the cover. I wonder if they'll run a photo of me. I try to think of one I have that I like enough to put in a national women's glossy. Nothing comes to mind. I'll have to get headshots, I realize, unsure how much that costs. A lot, probably. But my parents won't mind. They'll be so proud of me.

With little less than a month left until deadline, I know I really have to get on it. I need to sit down and pick a topic, whether it's the effects of divorce or how to deal with an inferiority complex or the raging debate over the cervical cancer vaccine: Should it be mandatory for high school girls and is that somehow encouraging them to have sex?

All the other interns have already started their essays. When I went to lunch with them yesterday, they talked about themselves the entire time. A chorus of *me me me me.* They went on and on about how well everything is going—their internships, their essays, their lives. My life is good but it's not *good* like theirs. Next week Hallie is getting a makeover for an article on pumping up your style, Lara is interviewing Rachel Bilson, and Beth is tagging along on a lunch with Candace Bushnell. It's so not fair. All I have are more press releases and query letters to read. Oh, and if I'm really lucky, I get to stuff some envelopes.

I returned to my cube feeling completely demoralized and determined not to repeat the experience. It's too hard on my ego. Maybe if I get a cool assignment from Lois or finish my Savvy Girl essay, I won't feel so mediocre. Until then, I'll talk to my fellow interns in the hall and stuff but no more lunches.

Jessica breezes into the reception area fifteen minutes later. She looks stunning in a twill skirt topped with a bright scrap of silk with bold, swirling colors that's fastened at the small of her back in a careless knot. I can't imagine having the poise to pull off something that daring.

"Sorry," she says, a little out of breath like she was running. "I got caught on the phone. I know, I know. Never pick up after six. But it was the West Coast and with the time difference, I'm almost obligated. Meanwhile, it was just the LA editor asking me some nitpicky little question that could have waited until tomorrow." She presses the down button and smiles. "All set?"

I stand up, teeter for a moment on my heels, and then walk to the elevator. I try to think of something small-talky and fun to say but nothing comes to mind. Then I notice a tattoo just below her left shoulder blade. It's some sort of Asian symbol. "Cool tattoo."

"Hey, thanks." She twirls around so I can get a better look at it. Her perfume floats in the air. Perfume! I knew I forgot something. "It means 'peace' in Japanese."

"Fun. Do you speak Japanese?"

Jessica laughs. "Me? God, no. I can barely speak English. But I love the Japanese culture. Very soothing and peaceful. I have several tatami in my apartment."

I don't know what a tatami is, but it sounds soothing and peaceful and I decide to buy one over the weekend. I too love the Japanese culture. Sushi is my favorite meal.

The elevator dings and the doors open. The car is

already full of partygoers, and rather than wait for the next one, we squeeze between a navy blazer and a feather boa. The thick scent of mingling perfumes coats the air and clogs my throat with its sweetness. Jessica makes some comment, which I don't hear clearly because I'm concentrating on holding my breath.

The second we step out, I exhale loudly, then inhale deeply.

Jessica does the same. "Okay, next time we take the stairs."

I laugh because she's kidding, or at least I hope she is. I can't possibly walk forty flights in my prized stiletto heels, which I wore to impress Michael and which already hurt my feet, even though I just put them on twenty minutes ago. The shoes make my legs look so fabulous—sleek and sculpted, like I go to the gym or jog all the time—I don't care about the pain.

At the curb, Jessica waves down a taxi with casual elegance. Even though there are lots of people waiting who have been there longer, she gets the first one that drives up. Now *that's* girl power.

As soon as we climb into the cab, her phone chirps (either "God Save the Queen" or Bon Jovi's "Livin' on a Prayer"; I can't quite tell). She looks at the display, then rolls her eyes. "LA again. I have to take it."

Jessica talks on her cell during the entire ride to the Four Seasons, which is just a dozen blocks away on Fifty-seventh Street. Traffic is light and we zip uptown in no time at all. The fare is eight bucks. Jessica takes out a ten to pay. I reach into my wallet and pull out my last twenty-dollar bill to contribute. I don't want to look like a slacker or a scrounger.

"Aren't you adorable?" she says as she opens the door. "Put your money away. Nobody's paying. It's on the company. Trust me, it's the least they can do."

Delighted with my first corporate perk (other than Evian, croissants, melon, brownies, Retin-A, and the snow globe), I toss the twenty into my purse and follow her into the hotel. The lobby of the Four Seasons is large and imposing, with tall marble columns and lavish flower arrangements. The hotel is lovely and modern and not at all like the one where my cousin Diana had her bat mitzvah. There are no gilt mirrors or crystal chandeliers or busy, patterned carpeting for hiding wine stains. As I walk to the elevator, goose pimples form on my arms, but I'm not sure if they're caused by nerves or by the air conditioning, which is turned up to arctic.

In the elevator, on our way up to the ballroom where the party is being held, I'm sure Jessica can hear my stomach growling. "Be sure to grab some sushi," she advises. "It's usually very good, and it goes quick."

The elegant ballroom is already packed when we arrive. I scope out the crowd for familiar faces but don't see Michael anywhere. Jessica heads straight to the bar, and despite her claim about the quality of the food, doesn't stop at the sushi station to get a hand roll or a piece of sashimi.

My stomach growls loudly, but I stick close to her. *Savvy*'s fashion editor isn't simply the coolest person in the room; she's also the only one I recognize.

"Here we are," she says with a satisfied wink as we finally reach the bar. Like at any party, the crowd is densest near the alcohol. "What would you like?"

Although I've fantasized about every moment of the party, I never in my wildest dreams imagined standing next to the bar with Jessica Cordero (with Michael Davies, yes). I don't know what to say. Since I skipped lunch, I should probably just get a Coke. But I can't do that. It's too embarrassing. Like: How adorable, the high school intern wants soda pop.

Maybe I should ask for a Bud. I'm used to drinking it and can easily nurse one while I get some food into my system. But beer at the Four Seasons doesn't seem right. The place is swank, and well, Budweiser is majorly unswanky.

I know. I should order a cosmo like Carrie Bradshaw. It's sophisticated, pretty, and comes in a martini glass (how cool is that?). But *Sex and the City* has been off the air for years. Maybe nobody drinks cosmos anymore. Worse: Maybe nobody ever did.

"Hey, I know. We'll get my new favorite drink," Jessica says, seemingly unaware of the turmoil her question created. "The white Russian. It's absolutely perfect: kitschy and fun. I'm trying to bring it back. I shot the January fashion story in Moscow. The layouts are beautiful. Lots of gorgeous people in fur-lined coats and hats—totally faux—drinking white Russians. A little literal, perhaps, but you do what you can."

I have no idea what a white Russian is. My friends and I usually drink sea breezes and screwdrivers and sometimes rum and Coke if someone's parents have just come back from Jamaica with a bottle. But a white Russian does sound kitschy and fun. I bet Lily will be impressed.

A minute later Jessica hands me my first white Russian. It's creamy and cold and delicious. Almost like chocolate milk.

"Yum," I say, surprised. I can't recall ever liking a drink so much on the first taste.

"See? That's what I'm saying. Any day now you're going to be reading about TomKat sipping them on the Riviera. The bartender didn't have cream so he tossed in Baileys. An excellent solution. I do love a bartender who can improvise. The substitution of Baileys, though, makes this a whole new invention: the tan Russian." She holds out her glass and clinks it with mine. "To the tan Russian. *Zdorov'ya.*"

She downs half her glass in a single gulp. I take more cautious sips, delighted by the flavor but still worried about how much I can take on an empty stomach. I tend to say stupid things when I get drunk, and I don't want that to happen here. Not with Jessica nearby and Michael somewhere in the crowd.

"What's zah-der-ov-yeah?" I ask, struggling over the word. I haven't even finished one cocktail yet and already I'm slurring my speech.

"Russian for 'good health,'" she explains.

I'm truly, *truly* in awe. Nobody I know can rattle off Russian with such casual confidence. They don't even offer the language at my high school. "You speak Russian?"

She laughs again, then takes another sip and gracefully dabs her mouth with a napkin. "Not even close. I just picked up a few things while I was there."

Jessica is so quick to downplay her talents that I realize she's the most accomplished person I've ever met *and* humble. Obviously she knows a lot more than she's letting on. How could she not? She's experienced so much. I bet that wasn't even the first time she's been to Russia.

Jessica finishes her drink and smoothly gets another one from the bartender, who smiles when she asks for a tan Russian.

She gives me a new glass, even though my old one's still half full. "This," she says "is what we call laying the foundation. Drink up, so we can move away from the bar and get some air."

I follow orders, which really isn't hard considering the deliciousness of a tan Russian. When there's nothing but filmy ice in my glass, I put it down on the bar and follow her to the back of the room, which is marginally less crowded. A waitress carrying hors d'oeuvres runs her tray practically under my nose, and I grab a salmon puff before they disappear. I take small bites, chewing slowly as if I'm happy to eat the same appetizer all evening. It's a total act. I'm completely starving and want to follow the salmon puff girl around the room drooling.

Jessica knows almost everybody present and she introduces me around. I feel very important standing beside her, even though I don't participate in the conversation other than to look fascinated by what anyone says, and when the publisher of *The Sporting Life* offers to get us both another drink, I immediately accept.

"I've dated him a few times," Jessica says when the man is out of earshot. "Pretty interesting for a businessman but that's not saying much. His kind is notoriously dull. I prefer to stay away from financial sorts. No creativity."

I agree wholeheartedly—the guys in the Future Business Leaders of America club are so boring—and try to think of some fun, interesting gossip to share. Unfortunately, all I have is Adele's wedding dress and we've already covered that. So I compliment her on her beautiful scarf.

Jessica laughs. "What? This old Pucci? I swear one of the swirls is a wine stain. I got it years ago while shopping for vintage with Kate Moss."

It's the first time she's mentioned her former life as a superfamous supermodel and it strikes me as the perfect opening to ask about her modeling career. But before I can get up my courage or even form a question, Jessica's intern flits over to air-kiss her hello. Erika Mulhville, the only daughter of publishing mogul Edward Mulhville, is a year older than me but she looks thirty-five. She's as tall as Jessica but much thinner and has the oddly plastic look of a Hilton sister. Everyone knows her stint at *Savvy* is a joke. She's applying to FIT in the fall and wants an industry job on her application. People say she needs every advantage she can get. There's even talk of her daddy donating a new auditorium.

Erika stays a minute before fluttering off again, which is a relief, as she ignores me the whole time. No, not ignore—she doesn't even see me. I'm beneath her notice. She treats all the interns and low-level assistants like this. She thinks she's such hot stuff because of who she is but we're not fooled. She was born into her identity. She didn't make herself like Jessica. I could be tall, plastic, and vacant if my father was a multimillionaire, too.

Sometime after my third tan Russian, I lose sight of Jessica. One minute she's standing next to me telling the photo editor of *Egoïste* about her trip to Moscow ("Such an old city with signs of lost beauty everywhere, like a grande dame; we must do something to help them"), and the next she's gone. The party is a total crush by now—you can't move without elbowing someone somewhere—and I squeeze my way through the crowd looking for her. I loop around the room twice with little success. I catch sight of her once but as soon as I get close to her, she disappears. Like a mirage.

The effort to find Jessica leaves me feeling dizzy and woozy, and I decide I need something to eat other than the stray salmon puff. The sushi spread is on the other side of the room, but I elbow my way there with little consideration for my colleagues. As far as I'm concerned it's every woman for herself.

By the time I reach the spread, my balance is completely shot and I have to hold on to the table to steady myself. I close my eyes and take several deep breaths. The room is buzzing loudly in my ears and I try to close out the noise. It doesn't work, so I open my eyes. Food, I think. All I need is some food.

I pick up a napkin with my free hand and immediately realize I'm going to need both for the sushi. So I finish my drink in three large gulps. Now I'm good to go.

The sushi spread is as impressive as Jessica said, and my stomach gurgles in response. There is salmon, yellowtail, and eel but no toro. I look more carefully for tuna belly while people around me grab sushi pieces like they're free nuggets of gold. Realizing I have no time to lose, I reach for another napkin and grab several pieces before they disappear. I devour them within a few minutes.

I instantly feel better. The dizziness is still there, but it's not as strong. However, I am still quite, *quite* ravenous. I go in for a second round, a little smarter now from previous experience. I skip the yellowtail—it's fishy—and get extra salmon. I also take two mackerel pieces. And a fluke. And some octopus. Which is a big mistake; it's totally chewy.

Deciding I've had enough for the moment, I find a quiet corner and stand there, trying to regain my breath. Fighting for dinner is exhausting business.

The evening is only half through but already I can tell that my first big corporate affair is a huge success. My outfit is perfect, I've spoken to several important people, and befriended Jessica Cordero. I've accomplished all of my goals except making sparkling conversation with Michael Davies.

Right. Time to get on that.

First I have to find him. This is probably the hardest part of the assignment, but it's only my third trip around the room when I spot him leaning against the baby grand piano. He has a martini glass in his hand and is chatting to a pretty redhead I've never seen before. Is she an intern? It's hard to tell. She seems too young to be an editor. Perhaps an administrative assistant? Uh-oh. An older woman.

Michael and the redhead seem to know each other pretty well. He has his hand on the small of her back, which is bare, and every so often she clutches the arm of his suit (gorgeous, by the way: pinstripe navy blue with a light blue shirt and swirly yellow tie) while she laughs.

This is something I hadn't thought of. When Lily and I ran through possible scenarios and opening lines—that is, after I convinced her he's not automatically gay just because he dresses well—we never once considered that he might already have a girlfriend. He's supposed to be single and into me because I'm cute, fun, and irresistible.

Or so Lily said. I'm not convinced about that. I mean,

I'm the editor of the school newspaper. We're never cute, fun, and irresistible.

Deciding another drink will make me cuter, funnier, and more irresistible, I search for the bar, which is harder to find than I expect. Because my head is spinning and the crush of people is so dense, I have a hard time finding it. When I tire of walking in circles, I decide that the sushi bar will do just as well. Then, as I'm piling salmon pieces on a napkin, I remember Lily's plan.

Luckily, Michael is just where I left him.

Without thinking too much about it (thought always gets me into trouble), I approach him from the left side. I hold out my napkin, which has an assortment of sushi in it. "Hi," I say, with a very casual smile as if boldly approaching guys is something I do all the time. "Trade ya."

The *ya* instead of *you* isn't in the original plan but it seems right for the moment. Michael, obviously on the same wavelength, turns around with a bright smile. The redhead looks at me with disdain but I tilt my shoulder, blocking her from my line of vision. What I don't see doesn't exist.

"Hi yourself," Michael says easily. He's clearly comfortable in any situation. That's such a good trait to have, especially in a guy. "I should have known you'd score big. You've got a talent."

I look down, thrilled by the compliment and *so* relieved he remembers me. There was a very good chance he would stare at me blankly and be like: Who are you? "I prefer to think of it as a skill," I say, hoping I seem at least half as smooth as he is. "So what have you got? I'm warning you, I'm not letting these babies go for a crumbly nut brownie."

His cheeks dimple. "Hey, it was your choice. The chocolate chip cookie was on the table, too."

"Also," I say as another condition occurs to me, "I'm not accepting yellowtail. It's icky and fishy. So whaddaya got?"

He leans against the piano and opens his hands. "Nothing."

"Nothing?"

"Nothing. Nada. Nil. I'm completely dry."

"Oh."

I have no idea what to do next. In all the scenarios in my head he always has something. Maybe not tuna or a brownie but something other than an empty martini glass and an irritated onlooker with red hair (wait, no; she doesn't exist).

"How about a different kind of trade?" he suggests, saving me from my own speechless stupidity. It's so embarrassing. Poor little Chrissy can only flirt when the helpful flirtee follows the prewritten script in her head (um, is that even flirting?). "I can get the next round. What's your poison?"

The thought of yet another tan Russian brings on a bout of dizziness and I immediately shake my head. No, that won't do. Alcohol is out. One more and I'm going to have to crawl home. But I like the idea. A different kind of trade. All I have to do is come up with a counteroffer. That shouldn't be too hard.

But my game is off. The confidence I felt in coming over here has been completely undermined by uncertainty. I stand there as still as a statue and sulk. Far from being cute, fun, and irresistible, I'm dumb, dazed, and boring.

As I stare at him with wide-eyed blankness, wondering how to get out of this without making more of a fool of myself, he smiles again. With dimples.

And then I know. It's right there in front of me.

"I'll take a kiss," I announce in a firm, clear voice, as bold as you please—and I'm not at all embarrassed. I've never, ever asked a guy straight out for a kiss (I've hinted once or twice), but now it seems like the most natural thing in the world. So natural I'm left wondering why I haven't done it before. *I'll take a kiss.* It's so incredibly simple.

Another smile—slow and lazy—creeps across his face. "Yeah?" he says, almost like a drawl. It's the most shocking thing I've ever said in my entire life yet he doesn't seem at all shocked. Just the opposite: It's almost as if he expected it to happen. But he couldn't have. Lily didn't know. I didn't know. Nobody did.

"Yeah," I say, taking my time. Just like him.

"Okay," he says, so softly I have to lean in to hear. I'm only a few inches away from him now, and I feel the warmth of his breath on my mouth a second before I feel his lips. They're dry and warm and he presses a little too hard (what's that salty flavor? Spanish olives?), but the kiss is still perfect in every way. Just as I'm about to close my eyes and never open them again, he pulls away. My equilibrium is off, and I have to steady myself by grasping his shoulders. We stare into each other's eyes for a moment, both of us so deeply moved words aren't necessary.

The feeling is so overwhelming, so intense, I have to look away. I drop my left hand from his shoulder and take a step back. I tilt my eyes down and notice the napkin with sushi in it. I hold it out. A deal's a deal.

He takes a piece of salmon. "Pleasure doing business with you."

Now I begin to blush. I can ask for a kiss without flinching, but a compliment heats up my face like a radiator in winter. All at once I'm self-conscious and awkward. For the first time in a long while, I remember the red-headed girl a few steps away. Her limbs are stiff and annoyed, and she's scowling. Up close I noticed her neat appearance. She's very put together: lipstick freshly applied, hair recently brushed. Every curl is in place, and I start to wonder what I must look like by now. A total mess. Obviously. I haven't glanced in a mirror since we arrived. My hair is probably a frizzy ball of frizziness and my lips are completely bare. I can't remember the last time I put on gloss. In the elevator? In the taxi? While waiting for my second drink?

Suddenly I want to be very far from here. I want to be home in my bed where nobody can see me.

The first stirrings of a headache begin to throb at the base of my skull.

I turn to the redhead and meet her frown head-on.

Even with the grimacey expression, she's still pretty. What is it with this company? Everyone is good-looking and perfect. Where do they hide the ugly people? They have to be around here somewhere. "I'm sorry. That was rude. I don't know what I was thinking," I say, holding out the napkin of sushi. There are four pieces left. "Please have some, too."

The girl turns up her nose at me. She actually tilts her head to a something-degree angle and looks scornful and dismissive. It's the *neatest* trick I've ever seen, and I'm about to ask her to do it again (and more slowly this time) when Michael laughs.

"Paige doesn't eat raw fish," he explains. "She says it's slimy."

"Slippery," she corrects. Her voice is low and husky, like she's been smoking for thirty-five years. Another neat trick.

Michael shrugs. "Slick, slippery, slimy. It all means more sushi for the rest of us."

Paige smiles tightly.

"Her loss," I say, trying for the wealth of meaning in a double entendre and somehow falling short. Perhaps because there isn't a wealth of meaning to extract. "Well, I've got more deals to make. See you around?"

"Definitely," Michael says.

Paige just emits more disdain. She's perfect.

I wave good-bye and head toward the entrance of the ballroom. It's been a good evening but now it's time to go. Other people must have had the same thought because the crowd has begun to thin. It's possible now to walk in a straight line without dodging to the left and right of oblivious Mulhville-Moore employees.

The lobby air is just as cold as before but it doesn't bother me anymore. In fact, when I step outside into the oppressive heat of the New York summer night, I instantly begin to miss the cold and wish I had a portable arctic air-conditioning suit that I could wear on scorching hot days.

Getting a cab in front of the Four Seasons is remarkably easy, thanks to a doorman who blows a whistle and raises his arm with authority. The ride to Penn Station zips by in a flash as I replay the scene with Michael in my head, and before I know it, I'm calculating how much tip to give the driver. The math is complicated, so I just give him a twenty-dollar bill and ask for five back.

I climb out of the taxi and take the stairs down to the concourse level because the escalator is moving way too fast for me to get on (it must be slower in the morning with all the commuters weighing it down). I smell doughnuts as soon as I reach the waiting room and realize with the grumbling of my stomach that I'm still starving. I can buy only five doughnuts with the money I have left (maybe I gave the cabbie too big a tip?) but it's just enough to get me one of each of my favorites: honey-glazed, Boston cream, jelly-stuffed, cruller, and plain, delicious chocolate glaze. I bring my box of goodies to the area around the departures display and kick off my shoes before sitting down on the linoleum floor. I cross my legs, take out the chocolate doughnut, and watch the letters on the black board flutter and twirl.

It's still early at a few minutes after eight, but for some reason it feels like 4 A.M.

I'm about to start eating my third doughnut (Boston cream), when I feel a tap on my shoulder. I glance up, hoping it's Michael—he did say he'd *definitely* see me around— and find myself staring into a vaguely familiar male face. Brown moppy hair, brown eyes, freckles across the nose. Name? Totally blank. Relationship? Not a clue.

"Hey, Chrissy," he says.

I wave, a friendly gesture that in no way lets on that I haven't the foggiest idea who he is. Do we go to school together? Probably not. I know everybody in my class. Could he be younger? Sure. But he doesn't look younger. He has a matureness about him. Another M-M intern? I lean forward to get a better look, but he's really tall and it doesn't make a difference.

He squats. "I know that look. You're trying to place me. Graham. We met a few weeks ago. I work with Lily."

Graham. Yes, Graham. He's a lifeguard. Works with Lily. We met a few weeks ago. Right. Where? It takes me a moment to remember. "Calypso Cataclysm," I say.

He smiles. It brightens his face but not enough. No dimples. "Right."

I try to think of whatever I know about him. "You liked them."

"I did," he agrees with a nod.

I smile and shake my head. "You're not supposed to *like* like them," I explain, happy to have a chance to fill him in. I can't remember why I didn't at the show. Maybe it was too loud. "They're a joke. Ironic."

"Okay," he says.

I'm glad he understands. "Okay."

I expect him to go away now that we've cleared up the little matter of Calypso Cataclysm's irony, but he stays and watches me. I should probably offer him a doughnut but I only have two and a half left and it's a long ride to Bellmore.

Graham stares at me for a moment, just long enough to make me uncomfortable, then sits down on the floor. "So, Chrissy, are you going home?"

Now, *that's* a silly question. I'm in Penn Station sitting on the floor directly below the departures board. But all I say is yes. "Yes, I'm going home, Graham."

He nods. "When?"

I glance up at the departures to make sure my train is still listed. Yep, there it is. "Soon."

Graham nods again, slowly this time. I don't remember him being so noddy the last time we met. "Soon when?"

I roll my eyes. Some people are so persistent. "8:35."

"It's 9:27 now."

I look at the clock on the board. He's right. It is 9:27. How'd that happen? "Oh."

"Oh?" he says, sounding like an echo.

Something about his tone makes me feel oddly defensive on behalf of the train. Which makes no sense. It's not my fault it isn't here yet. "I guess it's late."

Graham shakes his head. Finally! A variation. "No," he says, "the 8:35 left almost an hour ago."

See? This is why he bugged me last time we hung out. He thinks he knows everything. "It couldn't have."

"Why not?"

"Because I've been here the whole time."

He looks around Penn Station, which is pretty crowded for a Wednesday night. Commuters in their three-piece business suits are spilling out of the Friday's while a dozen or so people wait to buy tickets. A club kid in a superlarge hat stops at the Häagen-Dazs to buy a vanilla ice-cream cone. Mmm. Ice cream.

"Here where?" Graham asks when he's done with his surveillance.

"*Here* here," I explain. Was he always this dense? I can't believe Lily hasn't noticed. She usually likes them sharp. Her last boyfriend (or was it the one before that?) got a perfect score on his SATs. He's at Harvard now, studying organic chemistry. "On the platform."

"Chrissy, this isn't the platform."

Now he's speaking slowly, like I'm the dim one. I give him equal treatment. "Yes, it is."

"No, it's not."

I sigh deeply. I can't believe we're arguing about this. "If this isn't the platform, what are all these doughnuts doing here?"

My logic stuns him for a moment, and he stares at me, trying to come up with a rebuttal. But he can't. I mean, why else *are* all these doughnuts here?

"Okay, on your feet," he finally says.

"What?"

Graham stands and puts his hands under my arms. I don't want to get up but he's strong and practically lifts me up. I'm so surprised, all I can do is say hey. But with real outrage, like I mean it.

He sticks his hands into the pockets of his jeans and takes a step back. "Put your shoes on."

I looked at the Chinese foot-binding, torture devices and shake my head. I don't care how much ice cream he buys me, those things are not going anywhere near my feet. I walk in the opposite direction of Häagen-Dazs so as not to be tempted. Graham picks up my shoes, catches up to me, and loops his arm through mine. It's so wrong for him to be touching me like this (he's my best friend's almost boyfriend) but I don't have the energy to argue. Besides, the room doesn't spin quite so much when he's holding on.

"Where are we going?" I ask.

"To the platform."

I sigh loudly. Seriously: How many times do we have to go over this? "This *is* the platform."

He leads me through a doorway and down a few dozen steps. The air is thick down here and smells like a combination of fried steak fat and overcooked pretzels. My stomach roils. I close my eyes until the nausea passes.

"I mean, the track," he explains.

"But the track hasn't been posted yet."

"That's all right. Here's the train."

I step inside and immediately feel better. The air is cooler and fresher, though the faint chemical scent of lemon-flavored toilet cleaner lingers in the car. I sit down in the first empty seat I see, which is right next to the bathroom. Well, that explains the smell. The cushion is much more comfortable than the hard floor of Penn Station and I lean back. Graham drops the torture shoes on the seat next to mine.

"So you're good?" he asks.

I roll my eyes at the implied insult. This guy really thinks I'm stupid. "Yeah, I'm good."

He looks at me for a moment, then nods, satisfied with what he sees. "Okay," he says.

"Okay," I say.

Graham nods one final time, turns around, and walks away. I watch him depart the train before standing up. I grab my handbag and box of doughnuts and slide out of the row. The cool floor feels wonderful on my tortured feet, and it's with great reluctance that I step off the train onto the warm concrete. The second I do, he attacks me. Like he's a guard dog lying in wait for a thief to climb over the fence.

"Where are you going?" he snaps.

My patience with him is almost at an end but I struggle to be polite. It's the least I owe Lily. "Look, I told you. The platform."

He sighs. I don't know what he's so annoyed about. He's not the one being led through Penn Station against his will. "Where are your shoes?" he asks with such weariness I almost feel sorry for him.

I mumble a response: "I don't know."

Once again he hooks his arm through mine and guides me onto the train. The lemony toilet smell is still there but I don't say anything because Graham seems really upset. He finds a row he likes and tells me to sit down. Agreeable as ever, I take the cushioned seat by the window and lean my head against the glass. He sits in the aisle seat. Between us, to my amazement, are my evil stilettos. I *so* thought I'd lost those.

"Hey, my shoes," I say, delighted by their sudden appearance. I have no intention of ever putting them on again but I do feel a certain amount of sentimental attachment to them. They were present for the best kiss of my life.

Graham grunts and takes a magazine out of his backpack. He's reading *The New Yorker,* which implies he likes deep investigative journalism but I know better. He's just trying to impress people.

The trip out to Long Island passes quickly. After a while, the window I'm leaning against becomes hard and my neck stiff, so I switch positions and somehow wind up with my head first on Graham's shoulder, then his lap. At some point, he digs my ticket out of my wallet, but I don't notice because I'm sound asleep. I don't hear the conductor announce Jamaica or Lynbrook or any of the other stations.

The only thing I'm conscious of is the warm leg beneath my ear, and when Graham shakes me gently at the stop before mine, I'm shocked to discover the limb is connected to a person.

"Hey," he says softly, "it's coming up."

I open my eyes slowly, uncomfortably aware of the harsh fluorescent lights glaring above, and see Graham staring down at me with a concerned expression. His eyes are drawn together and his hair has fallen into his eyes, making him seem curiously unfamiliar. Like I've never seen him before. He's kinda cute like this, with the spray of freckles on his nose so close to mine and a half-smile on his lips. He doesn't have dimples, but right now he doesn't seem to need them.

He looks so kind and sweet and endearing that I say the first thing that comes to mind. "I'll take a kiss." The words are quiet and soft, more a light breeze than an actual statement.

Graham doesn't react like he's supposed to—no lazy smile, no drawled "Yeah?"—and for some reason, saying it now doesn't feel empowering like it did before. But nor does it feel entirely wrong. In the fluorescent glow of the slowly stopping train it simply feels like something that happened and then didn't happen.

He brushes the hair out of my eyes. "Hey, sleepyhead," he says, "we're there."

I take a deep breath, my mouth impossibly thick and dry, and sit up. I hold on to the seat in front of me for a full

73

thirty seconds, then stand. The headache at the base of my skull has spread all over my body. The train comes to a complete stop as I follow Graham to the door. Barefoot, I step onto the platform, which is still warm from the heat of the midday sun.

Without saying a word, Graham leads me to the escalator and watches as I carefully get on. The metal strips hurt my feet and I try to rest all my weight on the rubber strips along the side. It works for a while but when we get to the bottom, I fall. Graham catches me. Then he waves at a cab driver who's waiting for a fare.

"Almost there," Graham says to me gently. "Do you have money?"

I nod yes.

"How much?"

I open the box and look inside. "Two doughnuts."

He laughs for the first time all night and digs into his pocket. He pulls out a twenty-dollar bill, which he puts into the center of my palm and closes my fingers around. "You know where you live?"

I nod again.

"I want to hear it."

I mumble my address.

"Good. So I can leave you here?"

I bob my head for a third time.

"All right. Have a very nice sleep, Chrissy, and I hope it doesn't hurt too much in the morning," he says. Then he puts the torture shoes on top of the Krispy Kreme box, waves good-bye, and walks away. I think he's going to hail another cab, but he climbs back on the escalator.

It's only now that I'm in my hometown, a few feet away from a waiting cab, that I realize Graham doesn't live anywhere near here. His home is many miles away in Great Neck. Great Neck. It's like another universe completely. I can't imagine how you get there from here. Go back to Jamaica and transfer to another line? Wait for another train? How unfair. I am minutes from my bed and he is hours.

The full weight of what he did hits me then, and I start to run after him just as the cabbie honks his horn. "Hey, lady," he says, "do you wanna ride or what? We don't got all night."

Exhausted and in physical pain (my head, my feet, my neck), I look over my shoulder. The driver is standing by his car, which is already running, and pointing to his watch. In the glare of the parking lot lights I can see two other people in the backseat. Waiting. For me. So I stop running and call out thank you, but Graham has already disappeared up the escalator.

Don't Let a Hangover Hang You Up:
Surefire Cures

The next morning I'm appalled by so many things I can't possibly focus on a single one. Michael! Graham! Paige! Everything creates an exclamation of horror in my chest, and I lie in bed with my poor aching head under the covers. It seems so much better just to stay where I am.

But Mom has her own thoughts on the subject, and when I don't show up for breakfast, she comes charging into my room like an angry bull, opening my blinds (out, evil sunlight) and barking orders: Get up, get into the shower, get downstairs, get cracking.

I've already outslept my alarm clock, which gives up after the sixth snooze.

Mom waits until I'm officially out of bed—defined as standing with both feet on the blue carpet—and immediately starts tucking the sheet under the mattress, as if that will stop me from getting back into it. It won't but her stern look of disapproval will. I trudge slowly to the bathroom as she orders me to get a move on. My dad has already left and she'll drop me at the train on her way to the office. Darn it. Why couldn't I have angry, warring parents who want to get on my good side like Lily?

I take a very hot shower, hoping the heat will wake me up, but all it does is make me sleepier. I lean against the tile wall and close my eyes, the throbbing in my head intense and persistent, like a jackhammer tearing through concrete. My stomach is violent and angry, churned up like the ocean during a raging storm, and the thought of food, any food at all, even plain toast, makes me dry heave (thank god, it's only a dry heave). So this is a hangover, I think as I grab a towel. I didn't expect it to feel so much like the flu. The only good thing about it is that the pain keeps me so preoccupied, I can't think of how appalled I am at myself. (Michael! Graham! Paige!)

In my room the bed, with its tight hospital corners (my mom's insane), somehow looks even more inviting, and I try to ignore it as I stand in front of my closet, staring at my clothes. In my hungover state picking an outfit is amazingly difficult. I have just enough energy to care what I don't wear but not enough to care what I do. So everything I own is wrong. My favorite jean skirt: wrong. My new black capris: wrong. The purple cami I stole from Jackie when I visited her at Tufts: wrong.

Mom shouts impatiently that my oatmeal is getting

cold (who asked for oatmeal?), and I grab a bright orange T-shirt with a logo from a club on Barrow Street in the Village and a knee-length salmon skirt. The colors clash violently, which is what I like about the outfit; the violence matches my mood. I dress quickly and reach for a pair of Camper sandals. They're worn out and too casual for the skirt, but I don't care. They're the most comfortable thing I own next to sneakers, and I need all the comfort I can get. My poor abused feet are cut up from walking around Penn Station without shoes. I even had to remove a tiny sliver of glass from my heel while in the shower.

Looking as close to decent as possible, I trudge down the stairs, my stomach revolting as the first hint of cinnamon hits me in the hallway. Mom is on the phone when I get to the kitchen, and she waves me into a chair as soon as I enter. I sit down and stare at the full bowl of oatmeal, which is accompanied by a full container of strawberry-flavored yogurt. I can't possibly eat both. Heck, I can't possibly eat one.

As Mom chats with Aunt Emily about their weekend tee time ("Is seven-thirty too late? I think it's too late. Let's meet at seven"), I dip my spoon an eighth of an inch into the oatmeal and take a tiny taste. Eating is every bit as awful as I assume it's going to be. Worse: The cinnamon flavor is now in my mouth as well as my nose. Another dry heave.

I play with the yogurt, pretending to eat, and think about how to handle the situation. I could try being straight up with Mom and tell her I'm sick. I certainly look like I'm dying, especially in the unflattering glare of my bright orange T-shirt (hmm—maybe I should change). And it's not entirely impossible that I've caught some terrible flulike bug. After all, I've been working hard at my job, commuting every day in packed subway cars with people breathing and sneezing all over me, not to mention eating sushi from a buffet.

But even as I run through the different types of groans in my head (the ouch groan; the distraught groan; the soft, pained, I-don't-even-have-the-energy-to-groan groan), I know it won't work. Mom would never fall for it. She's been through this twice before with Jackie and Roger, and she knows what to look for. The party itself put her on high alert, and when I got home last night she grilled me with a ton of questions as if she were really interested in how it went. But I realized what she was doing and played it cool. I answered a few of the more harmless ones ("What happened to your shoes?"), then yawned like fifty times (all genuine) and went to bed. Tragedy—that is, the interest of a concerned parent, a speech on the evils of alcohol—averted. It would be a shame to undo all my good work by raising her suspicions with a sudden cold.

No, I'll have to suck it up. I don't know how I'll get through the rest of the day when breakfast alone is an insurmountable obstacle, but I'll just have to do it.

"Ready?" Mom asks, her ugly brown handbag (all those tassels!) on her shoulder. She holds up her keys.

I look down at the oatmeal, which is now cold and

gloppy. "Yeah," I say, carrying the bowl to the sink and dumping the leftovers in the trash before she notices I've barely made a dent. Mom's psycho about breakfast. She totally buys that stuff about it being the most important meal of the day, and she'd happily stand over my chair and watch me swallow bite after bite rather than get to work on time.

The ride into the city flies by. I'm no sooner in my seat than I'm passed out on the cushion next to me. I'm sleeping so soundly that the conductor has to shake me. I nod groggily at him and grab my stuff as memories of the night before flood through me. (Graham!) The details are hazy but I remember just enough to be completely embarrassed. And it's not just the asking-for-a-kiss part (god, what was I thinking?). Oh, no, it's the whole scene: being such a drunken idiot that I sat there on the floor of Penn Station eating doughnuts like a gross pig and missing train after train. I can't imagine what he thought seeing me like that. And then to have to go all the way out to Bellmore because I'm too drunk to stay on the train. He shouldn't have done it. He should have left me where I was to rot.

As grateful as I am to Graham, I hope never to see him again. I don't care how many weeks Lily dates him, I'm not going out with them.

Adele isn't in her cube when I arrive at work ninety minutes late, but her computer is on so I know she knows I'm late. I sigh heavily, disappointed that she's not hung-over and sluggish this morning, too. (Of course it was too much to wish for, but a girl can dream.) My desk is exactly the way I left it, with the stack of magazines to stuff front and center. I'd hoped that it had magically disappeared overnight or that Adele would show an ounce of humanity and send them herself (also too much to wish for).

I turn on my computer, drop my stuff on the floor, and head to the kitchen to get a cup of coffee, my second for the day. I usually take it light and sweet, with two packets of sugar and a good dash of milk, but this morning the harsh bitterness of black is the only thing I can swallow. The *Savvy* brew is especially strong, like nail polish remover or turpentine, and it feels as though it's peeling away my stomach lining as it goes down, which for some reason is oddly okay (less is more). I sigh, lean against the sink, and take another sip of coffee. Clearly, stuffing envelopes is pretty much all I can handle at the moment.

"Hey, chica," Jessica says, breezing into the kitchen with a bright smile on her face. She had just as many tan Russians as I did, or possibly more, but looks as effortlessly put together as always. Her hair is pulled back in a sleek ponytail, with perfectly curling wisps falling around her face. Her makeup is freshly applied but so natural looking you can barely tell it's there. And her outfit is another hot-off-the-runway selection. I don't know how she does it. "Great party, eh? I lost track of you toward the end."

I blink several times and try to wake up. "I cut out around eight," I say, more than a little surprised she's so affable. We were friends last night, sure, but things like that change quickly—as least they do in high school. Like: You

81

sit next to Sharla Winston on a class trip and you get along great (who knew the most popular girl in class even had a sense of humor?), and then the next day in the cafeteria she totally pretends you've never met.

"I left around then, too," she says as she grabs an Evian out of the fridge. I straighten up and pretend I wasn't napping in the kitchen. We walk down the hall together. "So are you going to do the Savvy Girl thing?"

I'm amazed she thinks there's any question. *Of course* I'm doing it. "Absolutely. It's an amazing opportunity."

She nods. "So how's it going?"

"Great," I say enthusiastically—perhaps a little *too* enthusiastically to hide the fact that the only thing I've figured out so far is the menu for my victory party. But I am working on it. I just have to narrow down my ideas.

At the end of the corridor I turn right, even though my cube is in the other direction. Jessica doesn't notice.

"If you need a sounding board, let me know," she says. "I've been here a while and have a good feel for the *Savvy* voice. I know what Georgie likes."

The offer is so amazing, I can't believe she made it. Imagine: Jessica Cordero wants to help *me* become the Savvy Girl.

"I'll definitely do that," I say, a little breathless.

We're now at her office and she pauses by the door. "Great," she says.

I'm about to thank her when the assistant fashion editor, Heidi Moakley, comes over. She's only two months younger than her boss but several years behind. "Hey, Jess, I've got to bail on that thing tonight. Glenn got tix for Springsteen."

Jessica smiles. "No worries. I'll find someone."

Heidi nods and walks away, and before anyone else can interrupt I rush to thank Jessica for her offer.

"It's nothing," she says. "Hey, do you have plans later? I've got a party tonight at the Hudson. It's for a designer from Paris. Michel Dupree or Dupré or something like that. He's up-and-coming and I promised his publicist I'd drop by as a favor. It might be a little boring but the food will be great—the Hudson does to-die-for baby lamb chops—and I absolutely guarantee we can have all the tan Russians we want."

There are a million reasons why I shouldn't go. One: I'm totally exhausted from the night before and have been dreaming of returning to my bed since the second I left it. Two: I couldn't possibly swallow more alcohol, let alone that devil juice responsible for so much recent humiliation. (Michael! Graham! Paige!) Three: I promised Lily I'd meet up with her to give the play-by-play.

But even as the word *no* forms in my head I say, "Yes, yes, I'd love to go." Attending a party with Jessica Cordero is too much of an opportunity to turn down. I can't believe she actually wants to hang out with me (take that, Sharla Winston). She's a supersuccessful British editor and former fashion model and I'm a regular old high school student from Long Island. It's amazing. Talk about being in the right place at the right time.

Jessica's wide, approving smile banishes any teeny-tiny lingering doubt I have that sleep should maybe be my first priority. "Fab. Let's meet by the elevator at seven. The shindig starts at six-thirty, but only the very polite and the very rude show up on the button. The Hudson's got a fab lobby bar we can hang out in if the scene is too dull for words."

I nod. "Great. Elevators at seven."

Returning to my desk, I immediately Google Michel Dupré—and it is Dupré, like café, with an accent. He's in his late thirties, with thinning brown hair highlighted with chunky stripes of red. His designs are bright and bold, with retro touches like shoulder pads, thin lapels, and high waists. The styles are fun and interesting, especially a pink embroidered blazer, but nothing I'd ever wear. I prefer my clothes snug so the extra material won't make me look fat.

While I'm reading reviews of his recent fall collection, I hear Lara, who is two cubes over, read the first few sentences of her SG essay. Her topic is body image. Although it's a variation on what I was thinking about, the topic makes me roll my eyes. Hearing it like this, I realize the subject has totally been played out, especially in relation to high school students. I mean, yeah, we all know we don't have to look like Mischa Barton to be pretty. Lindsay Lohan before the crash-and-burn diet is good enough.

I need something a little less personal and more world-stage.

Inspired by the thought, I close my browser and get a

copy of the *New York Times* from the recycling bin next to the conference room. I need to find something relevant, timely, and big.

I've barely read one story about stem cell research when Adele walks by and stares pointedly at the stack of magazines. Without her saying a word I close the paper, stick it in a drawer, and reach for an envelope. It's so not fair. Lara's working on her essay on company time.

The day passes slowly as I do menial, unimportant labor that has nothing to do with my SG column. Sometime after lunch, Adele swings by my desk with a fresh box of query letters. I slog through it.

At four o'clock I take a break and call Mom to tell her I won't be home for dinner. She's not at her desk, so I leave a message explaining about the party at the Hudson Hotel (oh, completely forgot: Must Google Hudson, too). Then I promise not to be home very late, probably around ten, and throw in an "I love you" because she's a sucker for that kind of thing.

As soon as I hang up, the phone rings again, and I look at the display, instantly recognizing Lily's number. I stare at it for a few moments, imagining all the terrible things Graham told her about my drunken stupor. And that humiliating, can't-be-regretted-enough request for a kiss! He had to mention that. I mean, what kind of almost boyfriend would he be if he didn't?

Sucking it up, I answer the phone.

"Howdy, stranger," Lily says in her usual forthright,

nonjudgmental tone. "I don't want to take you away from your very busy job. I know you've got a lot of stuff going on. But I just wanted to see what's on for later. I'm dying to hear how it went last night."

"You don't know anything about it at all?" I ask in complete shock. Even if Graham didn't tell her about the humiliation of the kiss request, he must have mentioned the humiliation of the five doughnuts. Or the humiliation of missing two trains. Or the humiliation of walking around barefoot. There was so much humiliation ground to cover. I can't believe he didn't go over any of it.

"How could I? You're too busy with your important city job to return my calls." Her tone now is slightly accusatory. And I can see why. I was supposed to ring her as soon as I got on the train last night. No, sooner: the second I stepped onto Fifty-seventh Street.

"I'm sorry about that," I say, genuinely remorseful. I should have gotten over my embarrassment and called this morning. "It's been a tough day, and I'll admit to being a little—" No, that's not right. If you can't tell the truth to your best friend, who can you tell it to? Certainly not your parents. I lower my voice. "I mean, I'm a *lot* hungover."

Lily laughs. "I'll take that to mean it was a great party. I can't wait to hear the details. Where do you want to meet?"

"Actually, about later: I'm afraid I've got to bail. I have another party. Ordinarily I wouldn't do this—you know, cancel one plan because something else came along—but it's a really big deal." I explain in a rush, feeling awful about blowing her off. It's something she never does to me, even with all her serial dating. "It's just there's this French fashion designer and he's in New York for the first time and there's this fabulous party at the Hudson Hotel in his honor and I've been invited to go with the fashion editor, so it's a really big deal."

"Hey, don't worry about it," she says. "I understand."

I let out a sigh, hugely relieved. "You do?"

"Totally. It's the fabulous imperative."

Lily always does this—says things like they're things. "The fabulous imperative?"

"Yeah, whenever you're invited to a fabulous party, you're obligated to go," she explains. "It's one of those rules they teach you in kindergarten, like look both ways before you cross the street. Personally I can't wait for the first time I bail on you because I've got the world's coolest party to go to."

"Me, neither. So we'll catch up tomorrow night?"

"Can't. Have a date."

Of course she does. It's Friday night. "How about Saturday? We could go shopping. You still need an outfit for your cousin's wedding."

"I'm working," she says. "But come to the beach and hang out. You've barely been there and it's already the middle of July."

The thought of spending an entire day lying on a blanket in the blazing sun and listening to my iPod sounds like heaven. "You've got it."

"Great. See you then."

Reading pitches is time consuming, and I never get another chance to pick up the *New York Times*. Most of the ideas are silly or ridiculous ("Dear Editor: Have you ever wondered what color your aura is and what that says about your ability to lose weight and keep it off?"), and I've no sooner put one of the few yesses to the side ("The ABCs of Antioxidants") than I look at the clock and realize it's five to seven. I shut down my computer, grab my bag, and run to the bathroom to check out my appearance. It's not a pretty sight. My cheeks are pale, dark smudges line my eyes, and my hair is like a wire whisk that's seen better days. I do the best I can with my limited resources—concealer, blush, barrette—and stand back to get a more complete picture. Despite my efforts, I still look hungover. The bright orange color of my T does nothing for my complexion, which is sallow even on a good day. God, what was I thinking to wear it at all, let alone combine it with this salmon shade? (And what was Jackie thinking to buy it for me? I always knew she didn't like me.) My sandals are hardly better. Flat and thick, they make my legs look like squat little tree stumps.

I can't go like this. I'm a total disaster: mismatched clothes, beat-up shoes, out-of-control hair. I should be locked up in a state mental facility, not hitting the town for a chichi party at an upscale hotel. What will people think when the fashion editor of *Savvy* walks in with a rag doll at her heels? I close my eyes to imagine the scene and see lots of shocked eyes and dropped jaws. Some people even point and laugh.

That's it; I'm not going. I can't deal with the humiliation (and I thought last night was bad). I'll just explain to Jessica that I have other plans that I forgot about. Really, really important plans. Like: dinner at the mayor's mansion. Yeah, she'll believe that.

The bathroom door swings open and Jessica walks in. She's wearing a short pleated skirt, striped knee-high socks, and a sleeveless tuxedo shirt in sky blue. She looks absolutely fantastic. Everything about the outfit works, even the ruffles on her top, and I'm more convinced than ever that I can't go looking like this. Jessica must have assumed when she invited me that I have a secret stash of glam clothes in my closet, not realizing, of course, that we cube dwellers don't have closets.

I dip my head to avoid looking at her. I don't want her to read the fear in my eyes.

"Hey, chica, I was just coming to meet you," she says, dropping her bag on one of the sinks and digging through it. She pulls out a tube of mascara and untwists the top. The wand is a bright, electric blue, the exact same shade *Savvy* promoted in last month's beauty feature ("A Whole Blue You"). When I read it, I thought nobody could pull off such an intense color (so eighties-wannabe-super-model), but as I watch Jessica run it over her lashes, I realize how wrong I was. On her it looks fabulous, of course.

I bite my lip and wonder how I'm going to get out of this without completely embarrassing myself. I know I should tell her the truth if I can't make up a convincing lie, but I don't want her to think I'm a completely self-conscious, self-absorbed dork. There are more important things in life than fashion (though maybe not at a fashion party).

Although I've already put gloss on my lips, I take out the plastic container and press my nose against the mirror to give myself something to do. Next to me, Jessica blinks a few times to test out her lashes, then turns to get my opinion.

"Too much?" she asks, fluttering them like a heroine in an old black-and-white movie.

On anyone else I'd say yes and hand her a tissue so she can wipe it off. But not Jessica. "Perfect."

"Excellent." She tosses her mascara back into her purse and pulls out lipstick. She puckers a few times, then rubs on a deep mauve color.

I watch out of the corner of my eye, taking an extra-long time to put on lip gloss because I don't want the moment to end. This is exactly how I imagine college to be: two girls primping in front of the mirror before a big night out.

I don't have the heart to tell her I can't go.

Jessica disappears into one of the blue stalls, and I stare at myself in the full-length mirror. I've gotten my hair some-what under control with a silver barrette, and from a few feet away, the circles under my eyes are barely visible. But there's nothing I can do with my outfit. I stand on my tippy toes to watch my calves take on definition. It wouldn't have been so awful if I'd bothered to put on real shoes this morning. Why did I have to be so obsessed with comfort?

"Fab outfit, by the way," Jessica says as she turns on the faucet to wash her hands. I drop to my feet, embarrassed to be caught in such a vain moment. "I love how those colors work together. Audacious. Reminds me of something my younger sister would wear. And Hurley's is one of my favorite hangouts. I go there all the time. Billy the bartender makes a fantastic amaretto sour, my drink du jour last month."

Although I'm not nearly as audacious as my unintended color choice would lead her to believe, I'm deeply flattered by her compliment. Jessica's opinion goes a long way to putting me at ease. Clearly she has no hang-ups about arriving on the scene with a rag doll in tow.

She holds open the bathroom door and asks if I'm ready. I take one last look in the mirror and say yes. Much to my amazement, I actually am.

DON'T GET BURNED:
Fun in the Sun
the **SAFE** Way

Lily doesn't know which party she wants to hear about first: the Mulhville-Moore or the Michel Dupré. The former seems like the obvious choice because she spent hours helping me pick out clothes and strategize. But a party for a French fashion designer's American debut is something beyond her imagining and she can't help interrupting herself to ask another question about it.

"So, wait, you talked to him?" she asks, shifting the tray to her left hand. We're at the snack stand during her one-hour lunch break. Because some oblivious architect had no idea how hungry playing in the surf makes giddy beachgoers, there are only seven tables for the entire beach, which is a quarter of a mile long, and we have to stand with our trays, waiting for one to open up. Lily is good at this. She does it every day and knows how to identify people who are almost done and stand over them intimidatingly.

"Yes, I talked to him," I say as the family at our table gathers up their garbage. The little boy is still eating his french fries, but his mom is wiping his hands like he's finished. "Dupré's a huge fan of *Savvy*. Like, he reads it religiously. And not just the fashion articles. He was able to list seven out of ten of Cameron Diaz's dieting secrets."

The boy's mother lifts the carton of french fries out of his reach, and he immediately starts crying. She gives us an apologetic look as she takes his hand and orders him to stand up. The father, looking on stoically, picks up the tray and dumps it in the nearby trash can.

Lily and I sit down. She looks at her watch. "Three minutes and forty-eight seconds," she says. "A personal best."

"I thought they had us with the boy and the fries. That carton seemed bottomless."

She shakes her head. "Nah. Always go for the young mothers. They care too much about what other people think of their kid's behavior. In another year she'll be too exhausted to bother, especially if she has a second kid. So, you were telling me about the designer. I looked at his collection online. Not bad. I thought we should buy a few pieces. A store in Manhasset carries his stuff, so we wouldn't have to go into the city."

"We can't buy Michel Dupré," I say, unwrapping my

hamburger as the sun beats on my shoulders. There's something very wonderful about being this warm and tired. "His stuff costs like zillions of dollars."

Lily shrugs. "Please. What are you worrying about? I've got my mom's credit card. We can buy anything we want."

"*We* can't buy anything," I say pointedly. "Your mom didn't give you the card to keep me supplied with designer clothes."

She opens a packet of ketchup and squirts it over her fries. "The card's mine now. It's none of her business what I do with it."

In recent months this has become a constant refrain in Lily's life, and I know, although she's never said it, that it goes back to the divorce. She's angry at both her parents and it's impossible to say which one pisses her off more: her dad for not keeping it in his pants or her mom for not sucking it up. Either way, she believes they've both given up the right to tell her what to do. They've already made a mess of her life; the least they can do now is stop making it worse.

I know this attitude isn't really good for Lily. Her parents are still her parents, even if they didn't try to keep the marriage together for her sake (this idea didn't even occur to them, another reason why she's so angry). Sometimes I think about sitting her down and presenting the situation from her parents' perspective—she herself would never put up with a guy who cheated on her—but she gets that kind of you-have-to-be-mature bullshit from counselors at school and from her grandparents. She doesn't need it from her best friend. My job is to listen to her problems and take her side and say, "Right on," when she's being oppressed. It's what she's always done for me.

Realizing I don't completely agree with her outlook on the credit card thing, Lily changes the subject. "So you're at the party chatting with the designer. Go on. What happens next?"

"He invited us to sit at his table. Jessica had to schmooze publicists and other designers, but I didn't know a soul so I stayed behind. Michel was great. He introduced me to a ton of people," I say, recalling how glamorous everyone was. It wasn't merely the clothes, which in themselves were stunning, but the poise with which they pulled them off. Nobody was self-conscious, everyone was beautiful, even the guys, and models walked around surveying the crowd from their great height, not even pretending to be like regular people.

From the moment we set foot in the private party room I felt inadequate—how could I not?—but it was such a bone-deep, encompassing feeling, I wasn't uncomfortable. Seeing these people in their glittering perfection was like flipping through the pages of *Vogue*. There was nothing remotely attainable about them. *Savvy* is can-do; it says: This is how you can be better. *Vogue* is can-not; it says: This is how you can never be.

It sounds depressing but it really isn't. In fact, it's kind of freeing. It lets you be you because you know you can't be anything else.

For this reason I was feeling pretty comfortable by the time we got to the bar. Jessica ordered two white Russians and my stomach lurched in response. As much as I wanted her approval and friendship, I was compelled by queasiness to admit that I couldn't possibly touch another Russian cocktail, tan, white, or otherwise. Surprised, she stared at me for the longest time, and, I, trying desperately not to squirm, became convinced I'd failed some very important test. But then she nodded emphatically, agreed it was time we changed our signature drink, and asked the bartender to recommend something fun, kitschy, and obscure. He quickly complied with a bright green concoction, which is how I wound up drinking four grasshoppers in two hours. They go down as smoothly as a tan Russian and have a nice minty flavor that makes you feel like you're doing something almost healthy for your body. Like brushing your teeth.

It's amazing how easy it is to get a drink at these private parties. They expect you to be either old enough to imbibe or old enough to handle it. It's so fabulous; I don't know why you'd ever bother with nightclubs and bars, where everyone looks at you suspiciously.

Of course I felt the effects of all that alcohol on Friday morning. Knowing I couldn't sleep late two days in a row without Mom's suspicion antennas going up, I set two alarm clocks for seven. I was sluggish all day and barely got anything done (poor Adele had to do some of her own work for ten minutes) but it was totally worth it. I can't remember the last time I had so much fun at a party, certainly not at Rob Zane's annual Bahamas bash, which he throws every February when his parents take off for a week in Nassau. At one point the owner of a chic Soho boutique sauntered over to our table wearing a T-shirt like me, and we immediately bonded over our casual stylishness. She gave me her card and insisted I drop by. I probably can't afford anything, anyway, but I'll definitely take a look, if for no other reason than the joy of telling the snooty salesgirls (there's always one of those) that I'm a friend of the owner's.

"Anyone famous?" Lily asks.

"I'm not sure," I say, laughing, a little embarrassed by the confession. I mean, it should be pretty obvious, right? Either you're famous or you're not. There's no in-between. "Everyone claimed to be famous but they weren't anybody I've actually heard of. Like: a seven-foot-tall model named Marisa something or other who's supposed to be on every billboard in Europe. Michel said, quote, 'You can't swing a dead cat in France without hitting her left nostril.' And there was a fashion columnist for the *Times*. Karen Curtain or Kerchief. Also: an important buyer for Barneys called Carl Heavesy. I remember his name because he was a big guy so I thought 'Carl Heavy Set.' Oh, and I met the fashion director for eBay. She's supercool. I mentioned I'd swiped a bottle of JLo's new perfume from *Savvy*'s giveaway table and was thinking about putting it up for auction. The perfume won't be out for months. She thought it

97

was a great idea. She even helped me come up with promotional copy. Not that I can remember any of it now. I knew I should have written it on a napkin."

"Ooh, it sounds fantastic. I'm so jealous. Did you take any pictures?"

I grin slyly and dig my phone out of my beach bag. "Of course. But only a few. I kinda got wasted and lost track of things."

Lily grabs the phone out of my hand. "Stop bragging."

She holds the tiny screen up to her nose and scrutinizes each photo. They're all crooked and out of focus and sometimes completely unidentifiable. I didn't want people to know I was using my camera so I only snapped shots when nobody was looking. The results are hilarious and Lily cracks up as she goes through them. She has a dozen questions for each one: Who's that? Were they nice? What's he wearing? Is that a hairpiece or a monkey?

"Great. Now show me pix from the anniversary party," she insists as she eats her last french fry and reaches for the hot dog that's been slowly baking in the sun. Lily is a funny eater: She has to finish one food item before moving on to the next. "I'm dying to see what this Michael guy looks like. And you haven't finished telling me what happened. So you see him talking to a pretty redhead. And . . . ?"

I fill her in on everything, even the really boring details that don't have to do with anything (well, the ones that I remember, anyway). She listens patiently, only interrupting when she can't help herself. When I get to the part about the kiss—a particularly good detail that I intentionally draw out—she squeals.

"You didn't," she says, eyes wide with shock.

I grin widely, enjoying her reaction. Talking about the kiss is almost more fun than the kiss itself. "I did."

"No."

I nod slowly. "Yes."

"You slut," she says, laughing. "I'm so proud."

I have nothing to add to that so I just giggle.

"So spill . . . What was it like?" she asks.

I open my mouth to answer and realize I don't know how to respond. It seems impossible to put something so monumentally immense into words. "Great. Wonderful. Perfect. And a little salty. I think he'd just eaten an olive."

Lily claps. She really is proud of me. Usually I get all nervous around guys I like but not this time. Maybe I've finally gotten over my hang-up.

We spend the rest of the hour discussing my next move. I have to do something. It's been three whole days since the kiss and I haven't seen him once, not even a sliver of his beautiful smile disappearing quickly behind closing elevator doors. Waiting until I just happen to bump into him isn't going to cut it. Lily says I have to be more aggressive.

"We've got to get him where he lives. There must be some errand we can invent so you can casually stop by his desk. Don't your two magazines ever interact? What if you dropped something off? Or picked something up?" Her eyes light up as she zeros in on a possibility. "Hey, I know. Tell him you're researching a story and need an article from the *Egoïste* archive. He can help you with that, right? Then you guys can neck in the dusty old stacks while you're 'looking' for the article. It's perfect."

The idea has potential, especially the part where we lock lips in the storage room, and Lily and I flesh it out as we finish our lunch. We get so wrapped up in our scheme that we don't even notice her hour is over until we see Graham hovering a few feet from our table with a tray.

"No rush," he says, balancing his tray on one hand. "Take your time. You just finish up your little chat without thinking about me waiting patiently over your shoulder. Watching. Judging. Tapping my toe as the minutes of my lunch hour tick away."

Lily laughs and assures him the table's all his. "And you don't have to wait until we're gone."

Although Lily mentioned in passing that Graham also had a Saturday shift, she said he's filling in for a guy on the other side of the beach so I assumed I wouldn't see him. I realize now how stupid that assumption was. It's a big shoreline, yes, but a tiny snack stand. Of course we'd run into each other.

Caught off guard, and still deeply embarrassed, I keep my head down. Cleaning the table strikes me as an excellent way to look busy, so I collect all the used ketchup packets and toss them in my hamburger foil. Then I stuff the wrapper into the empty fries carton. Lily, in a seemingly thoughtful effort to help, grabs her own trash, leaving me with nothing to do but look up.

Graham puts his tray on the table and sits just as I stand.

"No, you stay," Lily says, snagging my tray before I can even protest. When did she get to be so fast? "Hang out. I'm back on duty as of four minutes ago, and it's easier for two people to hold off the masses. When you're just one, some canoodling couple always asks if they can share your space. And they always sit on the other side and stare into each other's eyes like dumb animals, which makes you completely lose your appetite."

Graham shrugs as he takes off his sunglasses. "I don't mind the company."

Feeling trapped, I clutch my soda cup—it's mostly ice but I need something to do with my hands—and sink slowly onto the hard metal bench. Lily dumps the trays in the trash, waves good-bye, and jogs toward the ocean. I watch her disappear, feeling resentful and knowing it's not fair. Then I look at my hands, my half-chewed straw, the cracks in the old, white fiberglass table. Anywhere but up.

"Nice day," he says casually. Too casually.

I glance up, expecting to see him smirking at my expense—I'm so obviously uncomfortable—but he's not paying attention to me at all. He's emptying a packet of sugar into his iced tea. I take a deep breath and decide to say something polite and mature. Feeling stupid all the time takes too much energy. "Hey, I wanted to thank you for the other night."

He shrugs as if it's hardly worth mentioning but it *is* worth mentioning. His seeing me home was the nicest thing anyone's ever done for me, and suddenly it's very important that he know that I know what a hugely big deal it was.

"Seriously," I say, more earnest than I intend to be, "I don't know how I would have gotten home without your help. I'd probably still be sitting on the floor of Penn Station right now. It was totally out of your way. I can't imagine what time you got home. I hope your parents weren't mad. And even though you were doing me a giant favor, I wasn't very nice to you. I didn't thank you. Or even offer you a doughnut."

Now he flashes a smile and the simple act changes his entire face. His eyes, which are a regular muddy brown, sparkle with amusement and seem almost golden. Looking at him in the bright sunlight, I see a little bit of what I saw the other night when I opened my eyes on the train. He's surprisingly good-looking—not take-your-breath-away gorgeous like Michael Davies (I mean, seriously, who is?)—but nicely attractive in a way that makes you stop and think.

"I'm not surprised," he says. "You were pretty attached to those doughnuts. Even after you passed out, you were clutching the box like your life depended on it. I tried to pry your fingers away but it wasn't happening."

A hot blush, more intense than any I've ever experienced in my life, scalds my cheeks, and I look down, grateful that at the beach embarrassment looks like sunburn or heat exhaustion. I take several deep breaths and feel the sweat pool at the small of my back. I don't know why this is more horrifying than all the other things that happened that night, but there's something vaguely devastating about learning from a cute boy that you have a gluttonous subconscious.

Knowing I can't stand up and run away without making the situation worse (gluttonous *and* cowardly), I force a laugh. It sounds totally fake to my ears—way too enthusiastic and so stiff—and I cringe inwardly as I keep the smile plastered to my face. "You should see me with ice cream. I wouldn't let you within ten feet of me." It's a lame joke but it's all I've got to cover up the awfulness of the moment.

"I'm the same way. Especially with a Carvel ice-cream cake. When I was seven, I ate my brother's entire birthday cake while he and his friends were swimming in the backyard. Mom came in and found me on the floor in the middle of a puddle of chocolate. She still hasn't forgiven me for leaving her with twenty screaming ten-year-olds and no dessert."

While he talks, the heat subsides from my face. A cooling ocean breeze brushes my cheek as my heart rate slowly returns to normal. "That reminds me," I say as I reach for the striped beach bag at my feet. "I've got your twenty bucks." I open my wallet, hoping this is true. I had thirty dollars when I left the house this morning and all I've paid for is parking ($3) and lunch ($5.76), so I should have at least twenty-one and change. My wallet is stuffed with receipts and Post-it notes with reminders of things I should do, and I have to take everything out to scrounge up the proper amount. I hand him a ten and two crumpled fives. "Thanks again for helping me out. I really appreciate it."

Graham sticks the wrinkled bills into the back pocket of his shorts and simply says, "You're welcome."

I'm intensely relieved. The more casually he treats the good deed, the more horribly grateful I feel.

Smiling with 100 percent sincerity, I stick my wallet back into my cotton tote. A couple on the prowl for a table slows down when they catch me reaching for my bag, but then they see Graham's full tray of food and move on. Leaving the tote on the bench next to me as an added deterrent, I turn back to the table, where Graham is taking a deep sip of iced tea. With the third packet of sugar it must have finally passed muster.

I pick up my soda and also take a sip, forgetting that there's nothing left but a few drops of Coke-flavored, melted ice. I swallow.

The silence stretches on as he eats and I pretend to drink from a seemingly bottomless twelve-ounce paper cup. What was Lily thinking to do this to us? The only thing we have in common is her. And she's not here.

"So, good beach day?" I ask. Nearby a seagull lands on a garbage can. He squawks and dips his head, then starts nibbling on a half-eaten hot dog roll.

Across from me Graham wipes his hands on a napkin. "Depends."

I assume he'll explain on what it depends but in the

drawn-out seconds that follow I realize he's done with his answer. That's all I get for my amazingly polite, so-not-my-problem-but-let's-try-to-be-friends-anyway efforts: one word. *Depends.* Thank you, Lily. "I suppose from your point of view, a great day would be a cloudy one, so there are less people to worry about drowning."

This time he doesn't say anything at all—just puts down the napkin, takes another long sip of iced tea, and shrugs. Great: First short answers, now none at all.

Annoyed, I look away, toward the seagull enjoying his afternoon snack on top of the brown trash can. I don't need this. Seriously: It's my day off. I'm tired, both mentally and physically (my feet are still hungover) after a busy week at *Savvy,* and all I want to do is lie in the sun and flip through magazines, maybe go for a swim if I get hot enough. I've intentionally given myself a free pass not to think about Savvy Girl or anything challenging. Keeping Graham McPhee company doesn't fall anywhere on the list. It's already way too much work.

I'm about to make up a story about sunscreen and leave him at the mercy of canoodling couples (just what he deserves), when he says, "You know, it takes a lot of skill to play that bad."

I have no idea what he's talking about—zero, zilch, zip. Obviously he's in the middle of a completely different conversation. I don't even think I'm part of it. "Okay," I say, deciding that now's the perfect time to announce that I left my sunscreen at the blanket.

Before I can say another word he rushes on. "I know Calypso Cataclysm sounds like they're just tuning their guitars onstage but they really know what they're doing. Some of their chord progressions are brilliant. And one guy, the bassist, he's going to Juilliard. He's got a full ride and plays in the string quartet. I just wanted to . . . I mean, they're having a lot of fun onstage and kidding around, yeah, but they're not a joke. I just thought you should know that," he says before looking down at his tray full of food, which he's barely touched. He reaches for a hamburger and spends a remarkably long time unwrapping it.

While he fusses with the foil, I try to recall what I said to him about Calypso Cataclysm, but the memory is too hazy to make sense. One second I was sitting by myself on the floor of Penn Station eating doughnuts and minding my own business (perhaps a little too much, as my train had already come and gone); the next Graham was inexplicably walking me in circles around the platform. Everything in between is lost.

But even without the details I can figure it out. His comments are too pointed for me to misunderstand, and I realize that in my infinite drunkenness I must have said something that I've thought many times in my limited sobriety. Apparently I have more to apologize for than my subconscious gluttony.

"I didn't realize they were so skilled," I admit honestly. There's no point in pretending otherwise. My ability to judge music on the talent of the musicians is nonexistent.

I only know what I like to sing in the shower. "I'm sorry. I didn't mean to offend you."

Graham shrugs again as he takes the top bun off his burger and removes all three pickles. They're half covered with ketchup and so thinly sliced you can practically see through them. "You didn't offend me," he says casually, like he doesn't care at all. "Whatever you think is cool. I just wanted to explain that they know what they're doing. It takes a lot of skill to pull off that chaotic sound. That's all. But, you know, it doesn't matter to me. You have the right to your own opinion."

He's so determined to seem unoffended that it's obvious to anyone within a fifty-foot radius that he very much is. I don't know why he cares about what I think. My opinion of him and his likes and dislikes, musical or otherwise, has nothing to do with anything. Maybe he's afraid I'll say something to Lily about him being uncool or a geek. If he is, it's a total waste of energy. Lily's relationships are so short, I've stopped making decisions. It's a waste of *my* energy. Seriously: By the time I've figured out if I like a guy or not, she's already dumped him for the next one.

But it's clear that Graham doesn't know this about her. Her reputation for inconsistency (legendary at Roosevelt, although that only adds to her mystique) didn't follow her to the beach. How could it? No one on the lifeguard staff goes to our school.

Because Graham seems so incredibly clueless about his short-term status as Lily's BF, I find myself feeling bad for him. He's a really nice guy, a little earnest perhaps and defensive about music, but he deserves better than to be just another departing contestant on the Lily Carmichael dating show.

"That's cool," I say, deciding to stay at the table for a little while longer. The sun is hot on my shoulders, so I dig the Coppertone out of my bag and spread it on my arms. It's SPF 8, which I know is all wrong for a hot day. I should be using something stronger, like 30 or 40, but I want to get as much color as possible in the little time I have. The editors at *Savvy* would totally disapprove. They suggest you wear SPF 25 all the time, even in the dead of winter. "I still think the band is fun, even if they aren't *punk* punk. I think we should get them to play at prom, although the prom committee would never go for it. They like cheesy cover bands that play soft rock favorites and disco super-hits. It'll be all Celine Dion and Bee Gees."

He laughs. "It's the same thing at my school. The band that played my junior prom actually did a fifteen-minute Michael Bolton medley."

The thought of a fifteen-minute Michael Bolton medley is so horrifying, I shiver despite the heat. "How do you know so much about music? Do you play?"

Graham bites into the hamburger and chews before answering. "A bit."

I figured. His defense of Calypso Cataclysm seems pretty personal. "Cool. What instrument?"

"Mostly guitar, piano, sax. Some drumming but only the basics."

I totally expected him to play the guitar—I mean, don't all teen boys?—or maybe piano because whose parents didn't make them take lessons when they were seven, but certainly not both and a third one as well. It's a pretty impressive list. My only musical experience was flutophone lessons in third grade. And that doesn't really count because everyone had to learn it as part of music class. I sucked at following notes or reading music, but I loved making up my own songs. I'd walk around the house playing them as loudly as possible while our cocker spaniel, Tango, barked. It drove Jackie and Roger crazy and convinced my parents *not* to force me into piano lessons the way they did my siblings.

"You consider that 'a bit'?" I asked. His sense of accomplishment is totally skewed. "A bit" is supposed to be, well, a bit. Almost nothing. "Isn't that an entire jazz quartet?"

Graham laughs. "No, a jazz quartet is four instruments."

"I was counting the drums."

"That's 'cause you've never heard me play."

"Still. Three-quarters of a jazz quartet. That's a lot more than a bit."

He grimaces. "Not in my family. Everyone's very musical and plays at least five instruments, so I'm actually the slacker."

Although I have a cousin who plays two instruments

(violin *and* viola), I've never met anyone from a musical family before. In fact, I've never met anyone from a family with a single defining characteristic before. We Gibbonses certainly don't have one, unless you count hungry: One of us is always eating. "That's neat."

"Kinda. There's a lot of pressure. Mom plays the cello in the Philharmonic and Dad's a composer. They had me on my first instrument when I was two. And by 'on' I mean literally on it. It was Mom's cello. She was hoping I'd be a prodigy like Mozart, but I just crawled on top, then threw up on the strings. I've never gotten over it. Whenever I pick up a cello I feel queasy," he says, then takes another large bite of his hamburger. Obviously talking about it doesn't have the same effect.

I laugh and shake my cup, trying to melt the remaining ice. I'm thirsty but don't have enough money left after paying him back to get another drink. "Was she very disappointed?"

"Heartbroken," he confirms. "Until my sister came along and learned every string instrument in existence. She's such a suck-up."

"Siblings," I say, rolling my eyes. "They're always annoying, even when they're not trying to be."

"I know."

He falls quiet as he finishes his burger. I look over to the trash can, where the seagull is finishing the hot dog bun. As the last bite disappears into his mouth, he flaps his wings and flies away. I turn back to Graham and try to think of something to say. Music is a good topic. He seems to like talking about it.

"Are you in a band?" I ask.

"Yeah. Some guys from the city and I get together a couple times a week to play," he says.

Graham's band turns out to be the ideal topic of conversation, and we chat about it for the rest of the lunch hour. He's a little reluctant to volunteer information so I have to keep asking questions: What kind of music? What are you called? Do you have gigs? Can I listen to a demo? But he's happy to answer them in increasing detail (in order: grunge infusion, Happy Hunting Grounds, yes, maybe), and I even manage to get him to hum a few bars of a new tune he's working on called "Alison in the Attic." It sounds to me like a love song but is really about an old Fender gathering dust in a closet. I think it's quasi-autobiographical.

When his break is over, he walks with me back to the blanket, which is now in the shadow of Lily's lifeguard station. Although he insists that shade is much better for me (another *Savvy* reader?), he helps me drag the blanket to the other side of her chair until it's in full sunlight again. When he's happy with the placement, he leans down to brush sand off the corners.

"Don't worry about it," I say, realizing for the first time that he's a total perfectionist. I suppose you'd have to be with three instruments under your belt. "I like the sand. It makes me feel like I'm at the beach."

He gives me a look, laughs, and stands up. "I'd better get back to work," he says.

I wave the August issue of *Cosmo* in the air. "Yeah, me, too."

"Thanks for keeping me company. I know it cut into your tanning time."

I shrug it off. Since lunch turned out to be fun, I don't mind at all. "Not a problem."

"Cool. See you later."

Before he leaves, however, he tugs on Lily's ankle to get her attention and asks what she's doing later. When she tells him she doesn't have plans, he immediately suggests a movie, one of the summer blockbusters that's playing at the multiplex at the mall.

Apparently Lily doesn't remember that she and I have been talking for weeks about seeing the adventure flick together and accepts his invite.

Graham is ready for this and rattles off a theater and show time. "So I'll pick you up at eight. How's that?"

Perfect. It gives her just enough time to get home, shower, change, blow-dry, and eat dinner.

"Cool," he says, obviously delighted. His smile is now a mile long. "See you later."

Although these are the exact same words he uttered to me a few minutes before, they have more meaning when directed at Lily. He *will* be seeing her later. For some reason this leaves me feeling disappointed, and rather than trying to understand why, I decide not to think about it.

I'm at the beach, after all, and the sky is a gorgeously saturated shade of cerulean blue. The sun is beating on my shoulders, the ocean spray is a light sprinkle across my nose, and a brand-new issue of *Cosmopolitan* promises to put an end to bad hair days once and for all.

I have much better things to do.

Be a Boy Scout!
PREPARE DAZZLING CONVERSATION TO **WOW** HIM

I come in Monday morning and quickly breeze through the stack of press releases Adele left for the October "Stat!" page. Now that I've been doing it for a while, I know what to look for. Anything from a university or a medical association is good; anything from a company is bad. Manufacturers are constantly doing "tests" to substantiate their claims that their product is the best. It's not the unbiased research we pride ourselves on.

By 10:15, I'm nose-deep in back issues of *Egoïste*, trying to find a topic that Michael Davies would realistically believe I'm pitching to my boss. It's a huge challenge because there isn't much overlap between their interests and my department's. Most articles in *Egoïste* are either fashion layouts with superbronzed models looking bored to death in two-thousand-dollar jodhpurs (oh, wait, there's Marisa), or in-depth profiles of big-time power players on their way up or down the social ladder, or funny little pieces exploring the quirkiness of celebrity culture.

The best chance I have is finding a story about a famous fitness or diet guru, and I open each issue hoping to stumble across an exposé on Atkins or the South Beach Diet guy. So far I've had no luck. *Egoïste* is stuffed with gurus but the wrong kind: lifestyle, financial, fashion (apparently, there's a guru for everything, even astrology).

It's so depressing. At this rate I'll never come up with a reasonable excuse to visit Michael's floor. If I don't find something soon, I'll be forced to throw back my shoulders, march to the elevator, and stride over to his cubicle *with no pretense at all*. Entirely sober, I find the idea horrifying. It somehow seems worse than asking for a kiss.

Which, I remind myself, he immediately gave.

So he must like me, too.

But then why isn't he coming up with excuses to visit my cubicle?

Because he doesn't like me. I mean, let's be completely honest. He's probably forgotten I exist at all. Or worse: I'm some vague memory. He knows he kissed a girl between dry martinis but he can't for the life of him remember which one. And why should he? He had the pretty redhead to distract him. I bet he remembers her name. Oh: I bet he's on her floor at this very moment.

Obviously I'm wasting my time. I have much more important things to do, like work on my SG essay. The deadline is now twenty-five days away. The *New York Times* is just sitting in my drawer waiting for me to select a topic. If not stem cell research then maybe the war in Iraq. There are tons of things I can bring my fresh, seventeen-year-old perspective to if I only can find the time.

I really should give up this *Egoïste* thing now and focus on my important things. My future is at stake. Savvy Girl could set me up for life.

But then so could Michael. I mean, who's to say where things with him could lead? It's not like I'm about to start writing Christina Davies on the cover of all my notebooks (I am, of course, keeping my own name), but there's the very real possibility that we're soul mates. It's too soon to tell, although that kiss seemed like a good early indicator.

I reach for another issue.

Luckily Adele is too distracted by wedding stuff to notice how little work I'm doing. Her invitations (silver embossed on sunset rose), which she picked up this morning on her way in, have a catastrophic typo. The very first line says "Mr. and Mrs. Horrid Pare invite you . . ." It's supposed to say "Mr. and Mrs. *Harrid* Pare."

I think it's hilarious. Lois also got a good chuckle over it. Poor Adele looks like she's going to cry at any moment. It wouldn't be so bad if it were her own parents' names that are screwed up, but the Horrid Pare are her fiancé's parents, who already think she hates them (she does). They'll take it very personally.

I know it's wrong to laugh at other people's problems, but in this case I seriously can't help it. If Adele were nicer to me, I probably wouldn't be getting such a kick out of it. Or e-mailing it to everyone in my address book.

By lunchtime I'm bored to death with *Egoïste* magazine and its articles about people I've never heard of. It doesn't cover any fun things (like how Renée Zellweger lost the *Bridget Jones* weight) or practical stuff (such as the best zit creams for your skin type). And everything runs on for pages and pages and pages. Don't the editors know that people prefer blurbs and sound bites? Haven't they ever read *Savvy* or *Us*? I mean, *Egoïste* is not like *The New Yorker*, where the boring cartoon cover lets you know what you're in for. *Egoïste* has the hottest movie stars on the cover. It's so bait and switch.

I'm just about to give up when I find exactly what I'm looking for in last June's design special. An article about meditation rooms (the new must-have accessory for any stylish home, per the first sentence) features an interview with Dr. Carter Stefko, director of the North Star Wellness Center in Sedona, Arizona, and nutrition guru. Lois loves him. He's a total New Ager who believes that the mind and body work together to keep you healthy. Diet articles quote him all the time. He's big on antioxidants and lycopene and some things called omega-3 fatty acids, which he claims are "good" fat. (I find this suspicious. Seriously: How can any fat be good?)

I return the back issues of *Egoïste* to the *Savvy* library
and begin writing a script of possible conversation between
Michael and me.

ME (*casual*): Hey, Michael.

HIM (*eyebrows narrowed in confusion*): Hey . . .

ME (*as patient as one can be with a future boyfriend
who's forgotten her name*): Chrissy.

HIM (*light dawning*): Yeah, Chrissy. How's it going?

ME (*totally smart and professional*): Good. I'm just up
here working on an article about Dr. Carter Stefko.
You know, the nutrition expert from the North Star
Wellness Center in Sedona, Arizona.

HIM (*with no idea at all but trying to impress me—so
cute*): Dr. Carter Stefko, right. He's great.

ME (*still smart and professional*): *Egoïste* did an article
on him last June in the design issue, so I was hoping
to talk to the editor who worked on the piece.

HIM (*impressed with my reporting skills*): That's a great
idea. If you tell me who wrote it, I can probably get
you the name of the top editor.

ME (*neatly hiding smugness at success of superclever
plan*): Can you? That'd be great. The writer was Victoria Craft.

HIM (*typing into his computer, eyebrows knitted in concentration—also very cute*): Victoria reports to Cor-
nell Wright. His office is in the lifestyle department.

> Go to the watercooler and make a right. I can show
> you the way.
>
> ME (*with much sincerity*): Oh, that's all right. I don't want
> to bug you. You look like you have a lot of important
> things to do. I can find it on my own. So I make a
> left at the watercooler?
>
> HIM (*standing up, always the gentleman*): Nothing more
> important than you. And maybe after you meet with
> Cornell, we can run away together.

No, I think, shaking my head as I lift my fingers off the keys. That's a little too much. I hold down the delete button and watch the sentences disappear. So, trying again:

> HIM (*standing up*): Don't worry about it. And maybe after
> you meet with Cornell, we can grab lunch.
>
> ME (*de*-light-*ed*): Okay.

I reread the dialogue quietly to hear how it sounds and make minor alterations. ("Oh, that's all right. I don't want to *disturb* you.") When I'm happy with the smoothness of the exchange, I start a new document, brainstorming different possible scenarios that might come up and how to handle them. For example, when I get up there, Michael could be on the phone. Solution: Breeze past his cubicle like I don't know him, then find a discreet corner with good viewing angles and wait for him to get off.

I realize it's silly to plan out everything we're going to say to each other, especially when one of the participants doesn't even know he has lines. But doing so gives me a sense of control and makes me feel like I'm working toward an achievable goal. Any good reporter will write down questions before an interview and try to imagine her subject's responses so she can prepare smart follow-ups. It's journalism 101.

Plus: Typing looks like regular office work to anyone who happens to be walking by. And by anyone I mean Adele, who periodically glances my way, even with the major distraction of the disastrous invitations to keep her busy. Right now she's on the phone with her maid of honor, complaining about the printer. Actually, it only *sounds* like she's complaining about the printer; her real target is the Horrid Pare. ("Even if the Print Universe guy wasn't a flunky, he's probably never seen a stupid and pretentious name like Harrid before. Eli's father should have changed it to Harry years ago.")

When I leave at six, she's still going strong like the Energizer bunny. Having tagged every single person in the U.S., she calls her cousin in Paris, who was about to go to sleep. Not anymore.

By morning hurricane Adele has blown itself out and she's back to leaving assignments on my desk, like yet another folder of queries, which Lois gave her only seconds before. She doesn't even wait until Lois's back is turned.

I thank her for the work and begin straightening the

messy stack. I don't mind sorting through queries. It's fun seeing what kinds of ideas people have, even the crazy ones, and Lois notices what a great job I'm doing with them. She always compliments me on my choices. As soon as I get a free moment, I'm going to start pitching my own article ideas. It's clear now that nobody's going to assign me anything.

I just have to get SG out of the way, then I can focus on the magazine. I always have tons of ideas for the *Roosevelt Reporter,* from the quality of the cafeteria food to an interview with the stage manager for *Grease,* so I know it will be easy to come up with stuff for *Savvy.*

I put the new work to the side and open my Michael files, which are buried deep in my hard drive. *This is it,* I think, reviewing the script. I'm anxious and determined and ready. Well, just about.

A few minutes later I feel Adele watching me, so I switch to a press release and read it through. For the next hour I alternate between daydreaming about my Michael encounter and doing my job. It's exhausting, so much so I consider putting off the Michael encounter until after lunch. Or even tomorrow.

No. This is it, I remind myself. With very little effort at all, I could keep coming up with excuses not to do it until the summer is over and I'm back in school with all the boring stubble-free guys I've known since kindergarten.

At eleven-thirty I close all my secret documents, stand up, and walk to the elevator. My heart is beating at a crazy rate but I refuse to think about it. All I'm doing is asking about a guru named Carter Stefko. I'm a reporter consulting with another reporter. There's nothing special about that.

I'm so busy practicing my opening line that I don't notice Jessica until she taps my arm and says, "Hey, chica." I look up. She's brushing her silky smooth, blond hair behind her left ear and holding a bottle of Evian.

Even though I'm distracted, I manage to pull it together to say hello. Because I haven't seen her since the Dupré party on Thursday night, I thank her again for inviting me. "I had a great time."

She nods. "Yeah, it was fun. The Hudson always does a great job."

Although I have no experience on which to judge this statement, I agree wholeheartedly. Jessica smiles. I think she knows that I don't know what I'm talking about, but she doesn't call me on it.

"I've got another party," she says. "I was going to invite my intern but Erika goes to these things all the time and won't miss it. It's Stella McCartney's new line for H&M. Interested?"

Interested? I'm so interested I immediately forget I'm on a mission from God and stare at her in amazement. My jaw literally drops three inches. At the exact moment of my total dumbstruckness one of the guys from the mailroom turns the corner with a cart filled with UPS packages and Jessica has to pull me into the kitchen to give him room to pass. And still I stare at her.

I can't think of anything more fabulous than Stella McCartney. Even non-glamour girls know she's the hottest thing in the entire universe. Her last collection for H&M sold out in hours. There were lines around the block to get into the Fifth Avenue store. It was a phenomenon. People talked about the clothes for weeks. Half the cheerleading squad took the day off from school to go. Lily tried to talk me into cutting, but I had a social studies test that made up one-third of my grade and I needed to ace it. By the time we got to the H&M in Westbury a few days later, only scraps remained. Lily thought about buying a gauzy top with ribbons, but it had a tear down the left arm and the sales-girl refused to give her a ten percent discount (um, totally standard for damaged clothing). Lily has been waiting her whole life to wear Stella McCartney—I can't tell you how many times she's dragged me past her store in the meat-packing district—but she wants A-list pieces, not leftovers.

"I know," Jessica says, nodding understandingly, when I still don't say anything after a few seconds. "It sounds like a bit of a drag because it's in the Fifth Avenue flagship and not one of the hip nightclubs, and don't get me wrong, you're right. The space doesn't have any flow, there's hardly any room to move, and the sales floor is more densely populated with mannequins than some Midwest cities are with people. Trust me, you think you're talking to Judith Thurman and a second later you realize it's a dummy. But you should come anyway. Last time they served delish Bellinis and gorgeous crab cakes in the shape of little dresses. They dotted the tartar sauce around the neckline like it was a string of pearls. Very Jackie O via New England clam shack."

For the most part I have no idea what she's talking about. I might have seen a Bellini once during brunch at a Long Island diner but it could have just as easily been a mimosa (don't really know what that is, either). And Judith Thurman is a complete mystery to me. She could be an up-and-coming designer, a fashion reporter, or the president of FIT. Still, I don't want to seem completely out of it, so I say that mistaking her for a mannequin is easy to do. It's a shot in the dark but Jessica laughs.

"It's the neck," she agrees. "So long and graceful. Are you in?"

Once again my jaw drops. Am I in? You couldn't keep me out. "Yeah, sure. When is it?"

She twists the cap off her Evian bottle and takes a sip. "Tonight."

"Tonight," I repeat, thinking quickly. I have plans to meet Lily later at the mall to help her pick out an outfit for her cousin's wedding in Las Vegas in a few weeks. She so doesn't want to go. One: Who gets married in Vegas in August? It's a desert. The temp is like twenty thousand degrees. Two: She's supposed to go with her dad, who she's not talking to at the moment. Not that it matters. He's just going to cancel at the last minute like he always does: "business obligations" (we now know that means the secretary). Then she'll have to go by herself.

It kills me to blow off Lily when we have such an important expedition planned, but I know she'll understand. She's the one who explained the fabulous imperative to me, and if Stella McCartney at H&M doesn't qualify, then nothing in the universe does. And I'll totally make it up to her. I'll give her the goody bag. The whole thing. No matter what's inside. Even a dress.

"Sounds great," I say, wondering if they ever put clothing in goody bags. It seems pretty extravagant. "What time?"

"Let's leave here at six. We want to get there early before the crush."

"Great. I'll meet you by the elevators?"

Jessica says yes and grabs another Evian from the fridge. "Catch you later, chica."

After she leaves I stand in the tiny kitchen and squeal quietly in delight. I, Christina Suzanne Gibbons, am going to a party with Stella McCartney. It's totally unreal. I don't know what to do first: run to the phone to call Lily or run to the bathroom to see what I look like. Thankfully, I'm wearing my favorite outfit from the boutique in Nolita. It's the same one I wore to the anniversary party but with a blue cardigan to camouflage it. So far it seems to have worked. Jessica didn't notice.

Vanity wins (no surprise), and I duck into the bathroom for a quick inspection. For once the stalls are all empty, so I do a few happy twirls in front of the mirror. When I hear the door to the vestibule opening, I dart to the sink, turn on the faucet, and submerge my hands like

I'm casually washing them. I don't want people to suspect that I'm twirling happily in the bathroom during work.

Back at my desk I dial Lily's cell and listen to it ring three, four times. While I'm waiting for her voice mail to pick up, I realize I've completely forgotten about Michael Davies. I was totally on a mission from God before I got sidetracked by Stella McCartney. The party is superstar material but entirely off topic. I had one goal for the day, and even though I'm no longer sure of my lines, I have to complete it.

Not wanting to lose another second, I slam down the phone, take a deep breath, and walk briskly to the elevator. The truth is, I just want to get this over with so I can give my full attention to worrying about conversation with Stella McCartney ("So, is your dad dating anyone?"). I simply don't have enough energy to obsess over both situations.

Luckily, Michael is at his desk when I peek around the corner to take a look (scenario #1 averted) and he isn't on the telephone (likewise scenario #2). Taking these two developments as good omens, I stride over and say hello, per the script. That is: "Hey."

His fingers flying across the keyboard, he doesn't look up. Instead, he leaves me waiting while he completes his thought. It takes longer than I expect—he seems to be deleting as much as he's adding—and I start to wonder if I should come back after lunch. I feel stupid just standing beside his cube with nothing to do and no plan to implement. This situation *so* isn't on my scenario list. Epileptic seizure, yes (clear breathing passage, call for help). Maniacal typing, no.

Finally he finishes, hits save, and glances up. His beautiful blue eyes seem unfocused. He's looking straight at me but not really looking at me at all. "Hey."

My confidence has been somewhat shaken by the typing thing, but I know my lines and faithfully follow them. This is exactly why I drew up a script. "Chrissy," I say.

He blinks at me several times. "Excuse me?"

"Chrissy," I repeat, realizing too late how dumb it sounds. How dumb I sound. "My name is Chrissy. Chrissy Gibbons. We've met before. Remember? The Rice Krispies Treat. And the sushi at the . . ." But I trail off. He doesn't have a clue who I am. It's so obvious.

"Yeah. Right," he says.

An awkward silence follows as I wait for him to add something else. But he doesn't and I'm left scrambling to remember what comes next. It hits me eventually but not quickly enough to save my embarrassment. I feel the dreaded blush rising. "Carter Stefko."

This name means less to him than mine, and Michael stares at me, his long eyelashes blinking steadily. It's really disconcerting.

"He's a nutrition expert," I explain. "He runs the North Star Wellness Center. In Arizona. Sedona. I've never been there but I hear it's really nice. My boss went there for a long weekend a few months ago. She said the hot-stone massage was very good. You should try it." I know I'm babbling but I can't seem to stop myself. If only he'd show a reaction, any reaction at all other than that terrible, steady stare. "We write about him all the time in *Savvy*. Where I work. As an intern. I'm doing on article on him right now. He recommends a little healthy fat every day. I know, sounds like an oxymoron. But those healthy fats are the ones that aren't saturated. Like the kind you find in avocado. So I'm writing this article on him and I saw that *Egoïste* did an interview with him recently. Well, not really recently. It was last June."

I pause, giving him a chance to jump in. He doesn't. So I continue. Compulsively. "I was thinking that I could give you the name of the writer and you could tell me who wrote the story. I mean, worked on the story. The editor who worked on the story. The writer obviously wrote it."

Even my stupid mistake doesn't get a reaction. "Sorry, I don't know that kind of stuff. Maybe you should ask one of the editorial assistants."

Pawned off on an editorial assistant! He hates me. I just know it. "Good idea." I keep a smile plastered to my face as I try to figure out why he hates me. Because I babbled. Because I interrupted his work. Because I said "wrote" when I should have said "worked." "Where can I find an editorial assistant?"

"You can start with Paige," he says, tilting his head to the left. "She sits right next to me."

I follow the angle of his head and feel my jaw drop for the third time in an hour. Right next to him is the red-haired girl from the party. What rotten luck. She's the last person on earth I can ask my fake question. Having no idea how to handle this mess, I stand there, rooted to the spot. Seconds tick by.

"Was there something else?" Michael asks.

I'm so angry with myself for not having the imagination necessary to foresee something as disastrous as this that I can hardly think, let alone process his question. "What?"

"I'm in the middle of something"—he points to the computer—"so unless you want to ask me something else, I should probably get back to it."

Wow. Totally dismissed. Like a contestant on an MTV dating show. It couldn't possibly be more humiliating.

Struggling to hold on to a tiny scrap of dignity (the redhead girl is totally listening now; her head is down like she's engrossed in something else but her gossip antenna is way up), I force myself to look at him. His face hasn't changed. It's still blank and expressionless, like a movie poster for some independent drama about a middle-aged widower. It's infuriating. Suddenly his reactionlessness is more than I can stand, and I find myself willing to do anything at all to break it, even invite him to meet Stella McCartney.

Holy shit. I can't invite him to meet Stella McCartney.

But even as I know how wrong and stupid and flat-out catastrophically bad this is, I'm rattling off random details about the party. H&M. Bellinis. Judith Thurman mannequins. I'm not really sure what I'm talking about, but my

129

delivery is so good Michael can't tell. He's impressed with me. Better than that: The redhead's impressed with me. She's no longer pretending engrossment and is blatantly listening. Even I'm impressed with me. I sound so sophisticated chatting about Stella parties that for a minute I actually want to be me.

Michael doesn't jump at the offer because he's cool and wants to play it that way. But even though he says he can be persuaded, I know he's already 100 percent in. There's nothing blank and expressionless about his eyes now. I feel such a fabulous sense of accomplishment at breaking his impossibly steady stare that I forget that I don't have the right to invite him.

Giddy about my pending date with the supergorgeous Michael Davies, I float back to my desk. It's only when I'm sliding into my chair with a happy little, triumphant wiggle that I remember that he can't come to the party and meet Stella McCartney.

Oh, my god.

I'm too freaked out to sit calmly at my desk, so I go down to the surface and walk around Times Square for a half hour. After considering my options (what options?), I decide the only way out of this mess is a lie—a totally huge, outrageous lie that nobody would dare question. Like: I'm being rushed to the hospital with appendicitis. It's extreme, I know, but it'll totally work. Lying big is really the only useful thing I've learned in high school. From Machiavelli through Napoleon right up to Nixon, anybody who's anybody in history told the big lie.

Hallie is in the elevator when I get back and she wants to talk about Savvy Girl during the entire ride up forty floors. She's very excited about her essay. Her first draft is done and is with her high school English teacher, who has promised to give her feedback by next Monday. She didn't know if she should call Mrs. London during summer break but decided Mrs. London would want to know about Savvy Girl because it's so important.

I stare at her in amazement. Savvy Girl? I can't think about Savvy Girl right now. I have to figure out which lie is more believable—appendicitis or pneumonia.

Hallie doesn't notice my distraction and chats all the way to our cubes. It's funny how she thinks we're friends. As far as she's concerned, the Dalai Lama is one of our in-jokes.

There's an e-mail from Michael waiting for me when I get back to my desk. Heart hopping, I immediately click on it. The message is short but sweet:

On deadline. Have to turn in article to tyrannical editor. But am looking forward to party. Thanx for invite. See you later.

I read through it twice, ecstatic that he took the time to explain why he was distracted before. Obviously he cares what I think of him. Which must mean he likes me, too.

Otherwise he wouldn't be looking forward to seeing me later. Or tell me that he was.

Rereading the e-mail for the fourth time, I realize I can't possibly tell him I've got pneumonia (chosen for its misdiagnosis potential; a burst appendix is a burst appendix). If I break our date, I might be missing my one chance to be with him. There *has* to be another solution.

After much, much, *much* soul searching I decide to talk to Jessica. I'm probably making a mountain out of a molehill. Maybe it's no big deal for her to call the publicist and add another name to the list. It must happen all the time. And Jessica's a really important person. I mean, what's the point of being a tall, thin, beautiful, chic, British, ex-model fashion editor if you can't bring whoever you want to a party?

I walk to her office, incredibly relieved to have found a reasonable solution.

But once I'm in her office I can't say the words. Suddenly my request seems really, *really* embarrassing—not that I have a crush on a guy but that I'm so desperate for him to like me that I'd invite him to a party I have no right inviting him to. The bottom line is Jessica Cordero, one of the coolest people on the face of the earth, thinks I'm cool, too. She's so convinced of my massive coolness that she assumed my dumbstruck amazement this morning was indecision. As if someone like me could ever possibly think that a Stella McCartney party at H&M would be a drag. You can't buy that kind of rep. It has to come honestly, and by mistake. And I don't want to risk it, not even for Michael Davies.

"Hey, chica, what's up?" she asks when I stand in her doorway for a few seconds without saying anything.

What *is* up? "Nothing much," I say, thinking quickly. "I just forgot what time we—"

The second I come up with a believable cover story, the phone rings. Jessica glances at the display and raises her hand to stop me. "This'll only take a minute. Please have a seat."

My made-up question would take less than half that time, but I sit across from her and examine the objects on her desk while she talks. Like me, she has a snow globe of the Kuala Lampur towers, although hers is almost completely covered with small Post-it notes with scribbled messages. She also has several pictures of herself with other tall, gorgeous, British people (or American—it's hard to tell from a photo). Her week-at-a-glance calendar is opened to next month and is completely filled with names and numbers. It's the neatest thing I've ever seen. I don't have any sort of day planner but if I had as many things going on as she, I'd run to Kate Spade and get a beautiful bound leather one, too.

I would not, however, get the cast-iron candlesticks she has on her filing cabinet. Large and pointy, they look just like upside-down deer antlers. They're weird and scary. Like something that would come alive and dance in the moonlight in a Tim Burton film.

Jessica hangs up the phone as I'm scanning the top

layer of her in-box. It's filled with invitations and unopened mail. The card for the Stella event is right on top. It's classic and simple, with clean lines and beautiful paper, and I want to snag it to post in my cube. But that wouldn't be cool, so I stare at it for a little while.

"Sorry about that," she says. "Some days it never stops ringing, no matter how many evil looks I send its way. You had a question?"

"It's nothing," I mumble. Now that I've had time to think about it, my reasonable cover story seems a little bit unreasonable. My question is the nitpicky, annoying kind that e-mail was invented for. Only a total dork would ask it face-to-face. "I just forgot what time you said we should leave for the party."

"Let's see," she says, grabbing the invite. Good thing I didn't try to pinch it. "I think we said six, right? The party's called for seven but I distinctly remember Olivia telling me to get there early to beat the crowd."

She drops the invite on her desk bottom side up and I can easily read all the details. Olivia must be Olivia Cornersmith, the publicist in charge of the guest list. All RSVPs are to be called in to her by noon the previous Friday at the number listed.

"Right. Six. That's what I thought." With no reason to linger I stand up and move toward the door. I really don't want to lie to Michael about pneumonia but clearly I have no choice. I can't get him invited to the party and I can't tell him he's not invited to the party. A medical emergency is the only way out.

It's so depressing. Maybe I should just quit the internship and move to Bora-Bora. They don't have Stella McCartney parties there. At least I think they don't. (Note to self: Google Bora-Bora.)

Jessica tells me she'll catch me later and tosses the H&M card into her in-box. My eyes follow it longingly. It would look so great in a frame. And then it hits me: *The number is listed.*

Excited but not wanting to seem excited, I take a few steps toward her desk. I'm too far away to read the details on the invitation. I dart my eyes around the room, looking for something to comment on. I need an excuse to stay a few moments more. After a second I find it. "Great candlesticks, by the way. I've never seen anything like them."

Jessica smiles and looks at the terrifying candlesticks fondly. "Aren't they just the most fab thing in hunting chic? They were a gift from Georgie. I adore them."

"They are the fabbest," I say, not at all sure that the word can be applied to cast-iron antlers. They are so unfab. "Do you know where she got them? I'd like to get a pair for my parents' anniversary. They love hunting chic."

"I don't know where Georgie got them but Global Table in the Village stocks them."

"Perfect. Do you mind if I write that down?"

Jessica hands me a pen and a lavender Post-it and

rattles off cross streets. "They've also got a great website, if you don't want to bother going downtown."

I scribble the information carefully, then discreetly glance at her in-box. Olivia Cornersmith's telephone number is a few inches from the end of my nose. I jot it down as quickly as possible. My handwriting is so terrible that anybody looking over my shoulder would assume I was writing in code.

"This is great," I say, closing my fingers around the Post-it. "My sister and I have been stressing over what to get them. It's the big two-five."

"Good for them. Twenty-five years is great. My folks didn't last twenty-five minutes. Global Table has a sterling-silver pair of the candlesticks. You should give them a look."

Deer antlers, even ones cast in solid gold, would totally horrify my mother. She likes frilly things and flowers. But I promise to check them out as soon as I return to my desk. And because I'm feeling so guilty about all the lies I've just told, I actually go to globaltable.com and type "antlers" into the search field. Each candlestick costs fifty dollars. Wow.

I close the window and stare at the Post-it for several minutes, wondering if I've really got the nerve to call the publicist of Stella McCartney and add an extra name to the list. I mean, who do I think I am?

But at the same time, it seems like a pretty silly thing to worry about. The worst that can happen is Olivia says it's too late and I'm back to where I started.

Having decided to do it, I look around to see who might overhear the conversation and realize nobody's around. The area is completely empty. Everyone is at lunch.

If that's not a good omen, I don't know what is.

I dial the number and listen to the phone ring once, twice, three times. Great. It's gonna go to voice mail. Should I leave a message? No, a message could be incriminating. The publicist might play it back for Jessica, who would instantly recognize my voice and have me arrested for impersonating an editor. Columbia wouldn't take me and I'd have to go to Nassau Community College for an associate degree and work at a tiny small-town paper writing police blotter notes for the rest of my life.

I'm about to slam down the phone in a terrified, panicked rush when a person answers. "Hello, Olivia Cornersmith's line. Elton Valley speaking. How may I help you?"

The second he comes on the line, I realize I've forgotten to practice a British accent. How does Jessica say hello? I don't know. She always sounds normal and American until she doesn't.

"This is Olivia Cornersmith's line. How may I help you?" he says again, his aggressively upbeat tone making him seem like the sort of person who likes to say no cheerfully. I loathe him from the very first syllable.

"Hi. I'm calling for Olivia Cornersmith." My voice is freakishly high, as if all British people speak in falsetto. I just know he's going to call me on it.

"May I inquire as to what this is in reference to?"

The stiff formality makes me forget my own self-consciousness. This guy thinks he's so important. Hel-*lo*, your job is saying hello.

"The Stella McCartney party tonight at H and M. I have another name for the guest list."

"I'm sorry. The guest list is closed," he says, and I'm right: He's practically singing with glee. Clearly I've made his day.

"I know. But I was hoping she'd make an exception for me," I say, amazed at my own boldness. For a moment I feel like another person. Like—actually—Jessica Cordero.

"And who are you?" His tone is entirely flat now, neither singy nor songy. He's totally expecting me to be nobody, some assistant to an assistant who's naïve enough to think she can add a name last-minute. I hate him too much to give him the satisfaction.

I look around, make sure nobody is near, and say with force, "Jessica Cordero."

Immediately his attitude changes. Now he's all Mr. Gushy-Gush. "Oh, Jessie, hi. I didn't recognize your voice. Do you have a cold? Allergies? A new pair of jeans that haven't quite stretched yet? Anyway, no worries, honey. The guest list is never closed for a darling like you. Now what's the name?"

I roll my eyes. Elton Valley is such a phony, I don't know how he can stand himself. "Michael Davies," I say sweetly.

He repeats it back to me. "And that's D-a-v-i-e-s, right?"

I confirm the spelling.

"Fabu," he says. "I'll see you later, darling."

I hang up and stare at the phone, more excited to have put one over on the icky Elton than to have pulled off the scam of the century.

Feeling very pleased with myself, I open Michael's e-mail to respond with details about tonight. I want my message to be cute and clever, but everything I come up with sounds either silly or forced. Noting the stack of unread press releases still sitting in the middle of my desk, I decide that less is more. I get straight to the point, hoping unusual directness will make me seem busy, too. I write only:

Just added your name to the guest list. Party starts at 7. See you there.

He doesn't respond but I spend the rest of the day checking my e-mail and watching the clock.

PARTY DUDS:
Making the Most of Any Fete

By the time Jessica and I arrive at H&M my sense of superhero accomplishment has worn off and I feel anxious. In my ear I keep hearing Elton Valley's chirpy sign-off: "I'll see you later." What did he mean by this? That he'll see Jessica later? Or that he'll *see* see her later? There's a world of difference in the two. The second means he'll be at the party, seek her out, and mention something about her last-minute addition. The other means, sure, he *might* bump into her because they're at the same party but in all likelihood he'll probably only wave to her from the other side of the room as he scurries into the kitchen to tell the caterer to bring out more crab cakes.

The suspense is killing me. Waiting for the other shoe to drop, I eye all men for signs of Elton Valley–ness.

Although the party hasn't officially started, it's already in full swing at six-thirty. Olivia must have told the entire press corps to come early. As Jessica grabs two tall wine-glasses from the tray of a passing waiter, I wonder if I'll ever be able to find Michael in this crowd.

"Caipirinhas," she says admiringly. "That's a curveball. But of course Stella wouldn't repeat herself. Let's go see what she has instead of Jackie O crab cakes." She has to yell to be heard over the music, a blasting disco beat that is vintage H&M. Even when a hot, young design star isn't in the store, you can barely hear yourself think. Which is good. Shopping and thinking don't go together. You just wind up talking yourself out of things.

I nod and follow her as she darts through the maze of people and clothing. Jessica has well-honed party skills. She can move effortlessly through any crowd. Along the way she stops to chat with people and always introduces me. Sometimes they miss my name because the music is too loud. I don't mind being left out of the conversation. I like standing quietly and absorbing the glamorous atmosphere. It's so amazing. I've been in this exact same store a dozen times but it's never felt like the center of the universe before. So many beautiful people are here.

At one point, I even catch a glimpse of Stella McCartney herself behind a velvet rope in the VIP section. She's wearing a black slip dress with white stitching over the bodice. It's simple and elegant, and although it might be cut a little low in the front, there's nothing the least bit tarty about it. (Her ex-stepmother clearly didn't know what she was talking about.)

At five to seven I start looking for Michael. Jessica is talking to a *Glamour* editor and I'm a few inches behind her, resting against the banister, which gives me a perfect view of the escalator. I see him the second he comes up.

I don't want to interrupt Jessica's conversation but nor do I want simply to wander off. After a moment of stressing about it, I tap her on the shoulder, smile apologetically to the other woman, and say, "I'll be right back. I want to say hi to a friend."

She follows my gaze, singles out Michael, and winks. "Nice work, chica."

I turn away before she can see me blush. If only she knew how well I've really done.

Michael is getting off the escalator by the time I reach him. "Hey," I say, wishing a waiter would pass with a tray of drinks so I could casually and skillfully hand him one like a hostess. Like this is my party.

He smiles and checks out the scene. "Hey, Chrissy, this is some bash. Thanks again for inviting me."

I don't know what thrills me more—that he smiled, that he remembered my name, that he thanked me a second time.

Playing it cool, I shrug as if it's no big deal. "I'm glad you could make it. I know it was last-minute."

I wait for him to tell me he broke a plan to be here with

me tonight but when he doesn't, I cover up the weird silence with a question. "Do you want a drink? The caipirinhas are yummy."

His eyes are still bouncing around the room, looking at everything but me. I don't blame him. There's a lot to take in. "Sure," he says. "Can I can get a beer?"

Duh. Of course he wants a beer. Why would a guy want a silly girl's drink like a caipirinha even if it's yummy? (And: Did I really say "yummy" to Michael Davies? I'm so hopeless.)

"The bar's over there." I point to the cash registers along the far wall. "Follow me."

I try to navigate the crowded floor with the same effortless ease as Jessica, but it's impossible. People don't step to the side for me, and several times I have to stop and change directions. At one point I even follow him. My party skills suck.

Eventually we find the bar. There's a long line of people waiting to be served, but Michael smoothly moves to the front and orders a beer. When he offers to get me one, I tell him I'll wait for another caipirinha.

"Suit yourself," he says, stepping away from the bar and examining the beer's label.

I smile and look around for a waiter, expecting to see one a few feet away. Trays of shrimp and quiche circulate but no caipirinhas. It's totally cool—I don't *need* a drink— but I can't help wishing I had something to hold on to. Clutching a glass keeps my hands busy. Without one I feel an awful need to fidget. It makes no sense. I finally have Michael Davies all to myself. I should be ecstatic, not eaten up with nerves.

To calm myself, I try to think of something to say. It shouldn't be too hard. We both work. We're both interns. We're both writers. There must be a million things we have in common. Okay, now just think of one.

"How's *Egoïste*?" I ask after a moment.

Michael is still surveying the crowd so he doesn't hear me. I have to repeat the question twice before getting his attention. I'm not surprised. The music is *loud*.

"Good," he says. "You know, it's not all that but it looks great on a résumé."

It's hard to hear him because he's six inches taller than me and isn't leaning into my ear the way Jessica does. I try standing on tippy-toes to get closer and immediately stumble forward in my pointy shoes. Luckily Michael doesn't notice, and I steady myself without him realizing I'm a total klutz.

I wait for him to say more about *Egoïste*, and when he doesn't I struggle to think of another question. It's hard work making small talk *and* maintaining my balance. "What are you working on now? Anything exciting?"

He shrugs. "Everything they tell you about internships is true. Slave labor. I spent a week tracking down every bit of info available on Ryan Gosling for a major feature— I even talked to his kindergarten teacher—and then was ordered to hand over my research to the West Coast editor, who was doing the interview. It pissed me off. Everyone knows cover stories are fluff pieces hand-fed by publicists but the editor acted like she was writing *War and Peace*. I could have done it blindfolded."

I nod in complete sympathy. I've been having the same problem with Adele. I do all the hard work and she waltzes in at the end and puts her name on it. He's right. Total slave labor. If they're going to give us flunky work, they should pay us.

"How are the people?" I ask.

He dips his head and looks me in the eye for the first time all evening, but he doesn't bend down to my level. "No complaints. A lot of stuffed shirts who think they're writing fabulously clever pieces for *Vanity Fair*." He shrugs again. "It is what it is."

Although I nod again in agreement, his take on *Egoïste* surprises me. I've always thought of it as an upscale *Vanity Fair*, with edgier articles and more bite. However, I've never been able to read either magazine from cover to cover without getting a little bored, so it's entirely possible that I've got it backward. I must if Michael thinks it's the other way around.

"Yeah, it is what it is," I say, trying to sound as cynical as he. "*Savvy*'s all right. The people are okay." Actually they're better than okay. Everyone's pretty nice—except for Adele, the one bad apple in the barrel—but I don't want to sound too happy. There's nothing more annoying than a relentlessly upbeat person. "I haven't gotten to do anything really important yet, but they keep saying there will be great opportunities soon. We'll see about that." It's kinda challenging for me to sound so doubtful when *Savvy* has already delivered on its promise with the new SG page. But I don't want to mention that. If Michael isn't getting exciting breaks, then I don't want to, either.

"They're all the same," Michael says wisely, taking a sip of his beer and watching the escalator. It's after seven-thirty but people are still arriving in hordes. Pretty soon there will be no room to stand. We'll all be pressed against one another like inmates in an overcrowded prison. Someone jostles me from behind, pushing me against Michael, and my hand brushes his chest as I regain my balance. Hmm. Maybe stuffed to capacity wouldn't be so bad.

Although it's Michael's turn to ask me a few questions (and they can be about anything, not just my job), I concentrate on coming up with a few more of my own as backup. I also think of some *Savvy* anecdotes to have ready. By now I can do a pretty good imitation of Adele on a rampage. My impression of her yelling at the guy from Print Universe is spot-on (the secret is to accentuate the middle syllable or syllables: un-*ac-cept*-able, re-*puls*-ive, il-*le*-gal). But he doesn't say anything. It's not that he isn't interested, of course. It's just that the music is too loud and it's too much of an effort to make conversation. So instead he leans against the railing soaking up the atmosphere like me. We're so alike.

Michael finishes his beer and returns to the bar for another one. I try to follow but the crowd is so thick I lose him almost immediately. With a sigh of frustration I say excuse me to a pair of stocky businessmen in tweed suits who are blocking the way. They continue to ignore me, so rather than elbow them both in their paunchy, middle-aged stomachs I swing around to go in the opposite direction.

A man in a purple suit is standing directly behind me, and I bump into him with an *oomph*. I immediately take a step back and look up. He's tall, with a full head of silver hair and six diamond studs in his left ear. He's wearing a yellow daisy in his buttonhole. I stammer out an apology, which I'm not sure is entirely necessary. He was standing awfully close to me.

The man smiles widely, showing large, crooked teeth, and holds out a caipirinha, which, remarkably, remains intact despite my tackle. "Hullo, darling. Have a drink."

Without waiting for a response he slips the glass into my hand. Too surprised to protest, I wrap my fingers around the stem. It's a reflex. He then lifts his own caipirinha (also still full), tilts his head to the side, says cheers, and swallows the whole thing in a single gulp. I eye my cocktail warily, not at all comfortable taking a strange cocktail from a strange man. Not to be completely paranoid or anything, but I've seen this Lifetime movie: There are always roofies in the drink. I hold the glass to my lips and pretend to sip.

The strange man nods approvingly. "That's the way to do it, love. Genteelly, like a lady."

I grin. I can't help myself. It's a funny idea that sounds even funnier in his cockney accent.

"There you go. That's a beautiful smile. Have you ever thought of hitting the runaway? Of standing beneath the dazzling lights of Paris, London, and Milan? I can get you there, darling. Just say the word and I'll talk to a few people."

My heart flutters at the thought, and for a split second I see myself stumbling down a runway—and, yes, it would be stumble, since I'd be too nervous to walk gracefully—as dozens of flashbulbs blaze in my eyes. Of course I want to be an internationally renowned supermodel. I'd see the world, have gloriously sophisticated conversations with rock stars and world leaders, start a charity to save war-ravaged children, host a talk show, then walk away at the height of my success like Jessica. But I have more sense than to listen to him. Everybody knows that only dirty old men and Internet pornographers promise to make you a model. "I don't think—"

"I should have known you'd be in the thick of it," Jessica says, suddenly appearing next to me. She leans forward and gives the dirty old pornographer a kiss on the cheek, not at all wary of him. "How are you, Dommy? It's been ages."

"Excellent, darling. Truly and entirely excellent," he says, large and crooked teeth again in full display. "You're here in the nick of time. I was just promising to turn this charming young woman into an overwhelmingly successful model, and she was about to turn me down. I'm afraid she doesn't believe a word I say."

Jessica laughs. "That's because she's smart. Dommy makes that promise to everyone, even Madeleine Albright. It's his way of saying hello."

"No, it's my monumental ego. I say the word and Prada and Versace will fall in line."

Jessica smiles and rolls her eyes. "Like that ever happens."

"It worked with you, didn't it?" he asks smugly.

"Because I was already five eleven and emaciated." She turns to me. "This is the man who plucked me from obscurity and hasn't stopped bragging about it since."

"Dominic Edward Fothington the Third, also known as Dommy to my intimates," he says with a slight bow. "And you are?"

"Chrissy Gibbons," I say, and immediately realize how short and stubby it is. "Or Christina Suzanne Gibbons if I want to feel large and impressive."

His laugh is a high-pitched cackle, making him sound more like a barnyard chicken than an Internet pornographer.

"Dommy is the fashion director of British *Vogue*," Jessica says, making me realize that this is *the* British Vogue editor who discovered Jessica at a London flea market more than a decade ago. I take a closer look at him, searching for signs of— What? I don't know. Superpowers? A celestial glow? It certainly seems godlike to me that one man can take a teenage girl from nowhere and make her

the center of the world's attention. "Despite his seem-
ing smarminess, which I've pointed out to him a dozen
times"—here the fashion director in question simply smiles
and shrugs—"he's really a very nice guy. He always let me
keep the clothes from a shoot."

The topic changes then to fashion industry people I've
never heard of, and I watch them closely, fascinated by the
relationship. I wonder how Dommy feels about Jessica's career decision. Does he mind that she gave it all up after he'd
done so much for her? Was he hurt? Disappointed? Of-
fended? Angry? Sad? Happy? Indifferent?

He seems to be none of those things. Between him and
Jessica I see only genuine affection.

Eventually the conversation turns to the Stella collection we're there to see. Dommy starts listing a series of adjectives: divine, dazzling, stellar. Jessica goes next: inspiring,
humbling, blissful. Then it's my turn. I've never played this
game before and am stumped. Finally I come up with three
but they're pretty boring: gorgeous, stunning, beautiful.
Even Adele could have done better. Still, nobody says anything. Dommy immediately moves on to gushing over favorite pieces. Jessica is in complete agreement and says
nothing but "yes, yes" for the next ten minutes. I nod my
head wisely at regular intervals so it looks like I'm following the conversation.

Dommy has another party to go to and he invites me
and Jessica to tag along. "It's a very lavish affair in a seventy-
million-dollar penthouse apartment atop the Pierre hotel.

Three floors, fabulous view of the park. I know it's very gauche to mention dollars but I must, as that's the only reason to own a seventy-million-dollar apartment. You buy it and immediately put it on the market at a fifteen percent markup so everyone knows what it's worth. Otherwise, you might as well save a few pounds and live in a shack along the Thames."

Jessica says she'd be delighted to check it out, and although I'm extremely interested—I want to see more of their interaction, not the $70 million apartment—I pass. I can't skip out on Michael in the middle of our first date.

Dommy and Jessica dash to the VIP section to air-kiss the star of the evening, and I circle the women's department, looking for Michael. He's nowhere on the second floor, so I take the escalator down. Now he's easy to find. Even amid the crush of people, his gorgeous, tousled black hair stands out. As well, the cerulean blue of his suit (the exact color of his eyes, and doesn't he know it) is beautifully set off by the lime green satin dress of the statuesque blond he's chatting with. The girl has half a dozen inches on me, which must make her tremendously easier to talk to in the noisy store than short, stubby me.

But even as I make up excuses, I know it isn't about height or conversation. The divine, dazzling, stellar, inspiring, humbling, blissful blond girl is a model and I am not. Michael Davies looks like he could be a model and I do not. It's that simple. In high school it's cheerleaders and prom queens, and in the real world it's models.

Dommy's words repeat in my head, mocking me.

It's amazing how close I don't come.

"Hi," I say cheerfully. My smile is fake and way too bright. Anyone who isn't staring into the tractor-beam gaze of a supermodel could see that I'm about to cry. "You made a friend. Great. I'm going to take off. There's some party the fashion director of British *Vogue* wants to take me to at the seventy-million-dollar penthouse of the Pierre. I don't know anything about it other than my presence has been demanded." I'm being as name-droppy as possible out of spite.

"Sounds cool," Michael says, turning his pearly whites on me. He really has a great smile, and as hurt as I am, I'm not immune. Even though he doesn't want me, I want him, and it's on the tip of my tongue to invite him along. A party at the Pierre is the only thing I have to fight back with.

But I don't say the words. The blond is perfect, with delicate features, porcelain skin, and exotic gold eyes. The only way I'd stand a chance is if I suddenly and miraculously turn into Gisele Bündchen. And that's not going to happen.

To my surprise, Michael leans down and kisses me on the cheek. His lips are warm. "Thanks again for inviting me tonight. It's been fun," he says softly in my ear. Chills run down my spine.

"Yeah, it has." And it's true. Up until the part where he met a supermodel, I was having a great time.

He smiles again and straightens. His lips are no longer inches from my ear. "So I'll see you tomorrow?"

Since we've bumped into each other only once in three weeks, I strongly doubt that he will, but I politely agree. Then I wave good-bye and walk toward the stairs, which are considerably less crowded than the escalator. I don't have the energy or the desire to deal with other people right now. The giddiness of my earlier triumphs, from asking out Michael to putting one over on Elton Valley, has faded, leaving me totally exhausted. It has been a very long day, and all I want now is the quiet comfort of my own bed. But I won't give Michael Davies the satisfaction. It's silly because he'd never know the difference. But for some reason it matters. He has a supermodel, and I have the fashion director of British *Vogue* and a $70 million park-view apartment atop the Pierre hotel.

It's not the worst second-best in the world, I think as I spot Jessica and Dommy, but it does nothing to raise my spirits.

LIVING WITH
DEADLINES:

STRATEGIES FOR MEETING
YOUR OBLIGATIONS

Michael starts the charm offensive on Monday morning with a Rice Krispies Treat. He puts it on top of my computer and it's the first thing I see when I enter my cube. There's a little note attached that says, I OWE YOU ONE.

On Tuesday he leaves a dozen yellow tulips in a glass vase with a lavender bow on top of my filing cabinet. They're beautiful and delicate and everyone at the magazine stops to ask who they're from and why. (I got several happy birthdays and a festive cupcake from my fellow interns even though I don't turn eighteen until December.) I keep my answers vague because I don't know what the tulips signify. They're a conflicting message. I mean, they're flowers, so they're romantic, but they're yellow, so they're not.

My inability to explain them makes some people think I have no idea who they're from.

"A secret admirer?" Lois asks with a wink as Adele scowls in the background. (I don't know what her problem is: Print Universe sent her a fantastic bouquet of long-stemmed roses last week and they're still sitting beautiful and red on her desk.)

On Wednesday there's nothing waiting for me when I arrive in the morning, but at noon I receive an interoffice envelope with a pack of Hello Kitty chopsticks inside (whimsical: I like). I immediately call up Lily, even though she's still mad at me for blowing her off on Thursday. I didn't *mean* to forget to cancel our plans. It was such an incredibly eventful day that it simply slipped my mind. Too many things happened at once. I thought for sure Lily would understand.

I called first thing Saturday morning to apologize and reschedule, but she didn't answer the phone. She avoided me all weekend, which left me with a solid block of spare time to work on my SG column. I spent an hour reading the newspapers, jotting down possible topics: women in politics, steroid use, Title IX encroachment, racial profiling. I read Maureen Dowd's column on the abuse of presidential executive power and imagined my story being picked up as an op-ed piece by the *Times*.

The image is so real, I can see my name in black-and-white newspaper print. It looks perfect.

My sister came home at one-thirty for a surprise visit—a friend was coming down from Boston so she got a free ride—and distracted me for the rest of the day. She asked a ton of questions about my internship, then insisted we go to the mall to buy me some new clothes to keep up with my active social life.

On Sunday Dad dragged us to Old Bethpage Village Restoration, which is this cheesy outdoor museum with old houses from colonial days. We stood in front of an open fire in ninety-degree weather as some woman in seven layers of underwear and skirts made apple fritters. When she asked for a volunteer, my dad jumped forward. He loves this stuff.

As hard as I tried, I didn't get a single Savvy Girl idea from the experience—other than how lame outdoor museums are.

"I'm still not talking to you," Lily says as soon as she answers the phone. She's told me she's not talking to me several times in the last three days. It's how I know she *is* talking to me.

"Hello Kitty chopsticks."

Lily doesn't respond.

"Did you hear me? He gave me a pack of Hello Kitty chopsticks. They're pink and adorable." I take two out of the pack and try picking up an eraser.

"You know why he did that?"

"Yes, 'cause he knows I love sushi."

She makes a harsh buzzing sound in my ear. "Wrong. He did that because you caught him hitting on a model, remember? You're being played. It's called a charm offensive because it's offensive that he thinks you can be swayed by a little charm."

Lily's reversal on Michael has been stunning. The second I told her about the tall, gorgeous blond, she turned on him with such force I almost wish she wasn't talking to me for real.

I don't want to spend my days wondering what devious scheme he might be up to; I just want to enjoy the fun presents. And I don't see why I shouldn't. What possible reason could Michael have to apologize other than he's sorry for what happened? The only thing he stands to gain from the charm offensive is me, so why make the effort if he doesn't want me?

The part I can't quite explain, of course, is why he'd want plain old me over a blond, gorgeous model. I'm too old to believe in fairy tales, especially the one about personality trumping looks. I know what guys go for, and even though I realize they're all the same, I can't help thinking Michael Davies is different. He had beauty; maybe now he wants brains. (Yeah, like beautiful but boring isn't the oldest story in the book. Talk about your Grimm fairy tales.)

Happier with my take on things than Lily's, I tell her she's just saying that because she's still angry at me for ditching her. "For the hundredth time, I'm *sorry* I didn't call."

"That's not true," she denies emphatically. "I'm saying this because I don't want you to get hurt."

I don't want me to get hurt, either, but I can't see how that's possible. The guy is being *nice* to me. Why is that a bad thing? "Fine. But you *are* still angry."

"With good cause," she says. "I'd had a total shit day

and the only thing that got me through it was the thought of hanging out with you. And then you don't even bother to show up."

"I'm really, really sorry," I say with total sincerity. I know things in her life are pretty messed up at the moment and hate the thought of making it worse. Still, I can apologize only so many times. "I don't know what else to say."

Lily is silent for a moment as she thinks. "You can promise it'll never happen again."

"It'll never happen again. I swear."

"Good."

Relieved to be past it, I lean back in my chair and smile. Adele is at lunch, so she can't send me evil looks for doing what she does all day long. I have a dozen recently e-mailed articles that need formatting and logging but they can wait. The one thing I've learned about work in the last five weeks is no matter how much you do, there's always more. So why rush? "Tell me why you had a total shit day."

"Let's see. Dad informed me that he's bringing his girlfriend to Vegas with us for the wedding and Mom dragged me to a meeting with her lawyer. The guy's so sleazy. I swear he was looking down my shirt the whole time."

"He wants to bring the girlfriend?" I repeat, amazed. Lily hasn't even met the woman yet. Every time her dad tries to arrange it, she dodges his telephone calls.

"Oh, yeah, and get this. She has a daughter my age. He thinks we should be friends."

Just as I'm about to be properly horrified—the gall: to try to make Lily befriend the child of the home-wrecking slut who destroyed her family?—Lois comes over. She taps her watch three times. "Meeting now. My office."

"Hey, Lil, I've got to go. My boss just called a meeting," I explain. "Can we pick this up later? How about this weekend? We'll get you something really fabulous for this wedding from hell."

"Yes, let's definitely plan on a Saturday shopping expedition. I've got my eye on something and am in desperate need of a second opinion. Oh, and Graham's band is playing in the Village on Friday. You've got to come. You'll already be in the city."

Although I no longer think of Graham with exclamation marks and a mental wince, I'm not exactly eager to see him again. Something about him makes me uncomfortable. Maybe—and I know this is insane—it's because he doesn't make me uncomfortable. He's too easy to be with. He makes me laugh. (Seriously: That can't be good. He's Lily's *boyfriend*. I can just see the *Savvy* headline: "Friend or Ho—When You Have a Crush on Your Best Friend's Boyfriend.") Nevertheless, I agree to go to the show and promise to call her later to work out the details.

Lois's office is empty when I arrive but Adele steps in a minute later with a notebook. There aren't enough chairs for everyone, and Holly has to carry in her own, which she bumps against the wall several time. When she leaves a black mark in the glossy beige paint, she looks up to see if anyone noticed. I drop my eyes and pretend to be fascinated with my pen.

"Right," Lois says, coming into the room just as Holly puts down the chair and takes a seat. "We're behind in a few things and I'd like for us all to catch up right now. I know it's summer and it's hard to stay motivated with all that bright sunny sunshine in our faces so consider this your regulation Mulhville-Moore pep rally. Rah-rah. Deadlines rule. Now, what's going on with the Stat! section?"

"The write-ups are done," Adele says. "They just need polishing."

This is what she always says, and I'm amazed that Lois lets her get away with it. The logic seems totally flawed to me. I mean, if the write-ups were really done, they wouldn't need polishing.

Lois runs through her list of items to find out how far along each story is, and it quickly becomes clear that almost everything is on Adele's desk for polishing. She tries to blame Holly for not getting her the articles in time, but the editorial assistant is too smart for that and sent an e-mail CC'ing Lois every time she moved a story along.

"Right, of course," Adele says, seemingly calm and not at all defensive. "I appreciate the heads-up. It's just that sometimes you fail to send an e-mail when I return an article to you for a rewrite. I believe that's what we're talking about here."

Lois buys this hook, line, and sinker and reminds Holly not to forget to send out e-mails on revised stories. Holly mumbles okay as Adele innocently looks on. It kills me to say it but: Adele is good. She's so good I don't understand how she can't win over her fiancé's parents (I suppose she doesn't want to). I could so learn a thing or two from her about office politics. Knowing how to manipulate my coworkers would totally come in handy when I get a real job after college.

Despite Lois's businesslike attitude the meeting drags on for more than an hour, and I find my mind wandering as she and her full-time staff discuss articles for next year's issues. I know I should be contributing story ideas or, better yet, picking an SG topic once and for all, but I'm too busy obsessing over Michael. It's been three days and he hasn't come down. Is he waiting for me to go up? I've e-mailed him a few times to thank him for the thoughtful gifts. I've tried really hard to engage him in a chatty, fun exchange—one of the best ways to get to know someone is through their e-mails—but he's too busy. Maybe I should call him.

I'm so absorbed in the question of Michael, I don't realize Lois is talking to me.

Startled, I look at her. She seems pretty annoyed. I wonder how many times she's called my name. "I'm sorry. What?"

"How are you doing with Savvy Girl?"

Savvy Girl is in a really good place. I know exactly what I have to do and it's only a matter of actually doing it, so I tell her it's going great.

This answer is too vague for Lois. "Have you finished a first draft?"

Okay, so not *that* great. "Not quite. But it's almost there." And in a way it is. I have most of the weekend to work on it, so it's really just a matter of time. Which is what I mean by "almost."

Lois nods. "Good. Why don't you give me a copy on Monday morning?" She makes a mark on her calendar, penciling it in.

I'm so surprised, I drop my pen. It slides down my leg onto the floor. "What?"

"I'll take a look and we can talk about it in the afternoon, say four o'clock, which gives you almost a week to make the necessary tweaks."

She looks at me, waiting for confirmation of this excellent plan. I don't know what to say. Of course I'm thrilled she wants to help me on my column. It's a huge advantage I don't think any of the other interns are getting. But I'm nowhere near ready to hand in a copy to anyone, let alone my boss.

Still, I know it's for the best. The column is due nine days from today. I would have spent this weekend writing it anyway. There was never any way I was going shopping with Lily.

Darn it. I hope she won't freak on me for canceling again.

Of course she won't. She knows how important Savvy Girl is. She wants it for me as much as I want it for myself.

"Sounds good," I say after a long silence. Adele is rudely tapping her pen against the arm of her chair, as if actually counting the seconds. "I'd really appreciate your feedback. It's very kind of you to offer."

"My pleasure. I like your work. I think you'd make an excellent Savvy Girl columnist," Lois says. Then she stands up and announces we're done. "I'm ten minutes late for a meeting. See you all later. Holly, don't forget your chair."

Adele darts out of the room after Lois as Holly drags her chair along the carpet, which is too thick for easy chair dragging. I watch her struggle and even think about helping, but I don't want to move yet. Instead, I sit in the office and savor the moment. Lois thinks I'd make an excellent Savvy Girl columnist. Lois McQuilken, senior health editor and twenty-year magazine veteran, thinks I, Christina Suzanne Gibbons (yes, I am feeling very large and important), will make an *excellent* Savvy Girl columnist. It's so totally unbelievable that I almost call Holly to see if she heard the same thing I did.

But I don't. Because asking would be too much like a starstruck high school senior sighing over her first professional compliment, and not at all like an excellent Savvy Girl columnist.

Friday Night Rocks!
The Inside Scoop
on the
Hot Band Scene

On Friday at six o'clock, with one week to go, I finally settle on the perfect Savvy Girl topic: access to birth control. There have been dozens of articles recently about doctors and pharmacists denying women the Pill or emergency contraception because it goes against their religion. Eleven states (eleven!) are considering passing laws giving them the right to do this. It's called a "conscience clause," and Mississippi already has one. Can you believe it? It's actually *legal* for a pharmacist to pass judgment on his customers. In some cases women are forced to carry a baby to term because their pharmacist refused to transfer their "morning after" pill prescription to a store that's willing to give them the tablets.

It's the perfect subject: timely, worldly, relevant, edgy.

Now all I have to do is write it up in several perfectly formed paragraphs. With the whole weekend in front of me, that'll be a piece of cake. I'll have my first draft to Lois by Monday morning—right on schedule.

Feeling particularly efficient, I start a file called Savvy Girl Column and fill it with all the articles I've printed on the subject. Then I throw away the dozens of stories on rejected subjects. It feels good to have made a decision finally.

(My mom thinks I should pick something more personal that has to do with my day-to-day life, but I know everyone else is going to go that route. Mine has to stand out with its global reach and sophistication. And heaven knows *Savvy* doesn't need yet another article about loving your body or the challenges of dieting.)

Satisfied with my progress, I shut down my computer. Although six o'clock is a relatively early quitting time for magazine editors (Lois jokingly calls it a "half day"), it's late for a Friday in the summer and I'm one of the few people left in the office. Lois dashed out at two to catch the train to East Hampton. Adele waited long enough for Lois's elevator to reach the ground floor, then cut out herself. Holly repeated the routine, giving Adele an extra few minutes to clear the building before calling it a day. I would have followed a second later but needed the time to work on my column. And seeing as I've chosen the perfect topic, the time was obviously well spent.

I'm putting my iPod into my bag when Jessica breezes by. She's carrying several folders and leaves one on her assistant's desk. She jots a quick note on a Post-it, which she attaches to the file. Then she turns around and sees me.

"Hey, chica, what are you still doing here?" she asks, leaning her shoulder against the cubicle wall. "It's Friday. Half the staff didn't even bother coming in and the rest sneaked out after lunch."

"Working on Savvy Girl," I explain as I hold up the folder. I don't mention that, with plans in the city later, I have to stick around anyway. I like projecting the image of responsible journalist.

Jessica is immediately impressed. "Good for you. How's it going?"

I put my folder into my bag. "Draft number one is seconds away from completion." Again: This isn't the whole truth but it makes me feel good.

"Fabulous. I'm glad you're taking this seriously. Savvy Girl is one of those rare, once-in-a-lifetime opportunities. Make the most of it."

Her tone is so emphatic, so filled with conviction that I know immediately she's talking from personal experience. Dommy Fothington saw her face in a crowd in Camden Town and she made the most of it. That's how life works.

But she didn't quite. At some point she stopped making the most of it and made her life something else entirely. And that's what I want to know more about. Even though it's none of my business, I can't stop myself from prying. This might be my only chance. "Hey, can I ask you something?"

"Sure," she says. Everybody always says sure because they don't know yet what the question is.

I take a deep breath and exhale. "Why did you give it up?"

Jessica doesn't answer right away. At first I think she has no idea what I'm talking about. *Give what up?* she's wondering. Then I worry that she's annoyed. Who am I to ask her anything? I'm not her friend. I'm just some dinky intern she took to a few parties.

But it turns out it's neither.

"My sister," she says simply.

Jessica pushes my back issues of the *New York Times* to the side and slides onto my desk. She answers easily, not at all self-conscious about talking about something so personal. "Josie's younger than me, about your age, a little older. She actually looks a bit like you. The wavy hair, the green eyes. Highly impressionable. When I got my first cover—British *Vogue,* of course, God love Dommy—she was ten and beautiful. Eager. Outgoing. Optimistic. By the time she was fourteen she was obsessed with her weight. Emaciated. Drawn. Tired. Distracted. She stopped eating. Drank tons of coffee. Worked out for two hours every day. Started smoking. She would come to London for the weekend and we'd practice our runway walks together. It was great. And then one day I looked at her—fourteen years old, a cigarette between her fingers, a cup of Starbucks in her hand—and saw myself. In a flash I got it: She was me. And it wasn't beautiful. I realized then and there that this wasn't the example I wanted to set, and quit."

Her story is so amazing, I can't think of a single thing to say. I try to imagine Jackie giving up her career to protect me. It's inconceivable. Not that she doesn't love me—she and I get along great and she lets me hang with her friends in Boston a few times a year—but she has her own life and I have mine.

My look must have conveyed complete astonishment because Jessica laughs. "Don't be too impressed. I quit modeling, not fashion. I use my connections constantly. I only got this job because I know people. You have no idea what a recommendation from John Galliano does for your career."

Although Jessica's 100 percent sincere, I know she's just trying to play down her accomplishments. She does this all the time. It's like she's embarrassed by success. But rather than gush like a breathless teenage fan, I ask how her sister is doing now. It seems like an adult question.

"About to start her first year at Oxford and completely freaking. She's not sure if she wants to major in economics, history, or Spanish," she says proudly. "She's still on the waifish side but she's stopped smoking and eats balanced meals. I couldn't quite get her to kick the coffee habit. She's a sucker for a good macchiato."

The affection in her voice is so clear. I wonder if Jackie ever talks about me like that. "Your sister sounds really cool."

"Oh, she is. Too cool for me these days. She was supposed to fly over for my birthday but canceled at the last minute because her boyfriend invited her to his family's château in the Loire. New York cannot compete."

"That's a tough one," I admit, desperately envious that I don't have to make difficult decisions like that. I can't imagine choosing between two countries. Sometimes when we go out to dinner, my parents let me pick the restaurant. It doesn't compare.

Jessica smiles. "Not for Josie. She might have hesitated for, oh, maybe two seconds. But I'm fine with it. I'm having a big blowout anyway. It's not every day a girl hits a quarter of a century. You should come."

The subject change is so swift, it takes me a moment to realize she's inviting me to her birthday party. When the truth sinks in, I'm speechless. Jessica Cordero wants to hang with me *outside of work*. This is huge. I can hardly speak, I'm so excited.

But I struggle to play it cool. "Sure. When is it?"

"Tomorrow night. Mariposa on Houston. Doors open at eight but the party doesn't start until ten."

Ten is perfect. It leaves me all day to work on Savvy Girl. I won't have to leave for the city until eight-thirty, which is plenty of time to finish the first draft. I'll revise on Sunday and hand in a *second* draft to Lois on Monday.

"Sounds good," I say. "Count me in."

Jessica stands up. "Excellent. It should be a fun time. And no presents, please. I can't stand writing thank-you notes."

I promise I won't bring anything even as I try to think of the perfect gift. Shopping for Jessica Cordero won't be easy since she already has everything. I'll have to find something small but thoughtful like a book (which is really all I can afford, anyway).

After Jessica returns to her office—I completely forgot to ask why she is there so late, too—I turn off my light, put my bag on my shoulder, and leave. By the time I get to West Fourth Street it's seven-thirty and all I have time for is a burger and fries at the takeout place next door to the bar where the show is. I eat quickly, flipping through the *Village Voice* to see if Graham's band is listed (it's not).

To my disappointment, Lily's not at the bar when I arrive and I consider going back to the burger joint for another fifteen minutes. I hate sitting by myself in strange places, but I muster the nerve to grab a stool. If I feel really stupid, I can always take out a magazine and pretend to read.

The bartender, an old guy with gray-streaked hair, comes right over and requests my ID. He stares at it for several seconds, trying to figure out what's wrong with it (the governor of Virginia's name is misspelled) before losing interest. He puts my license on the bar and asks what I want. I order a Corona and look around. Onstage, Graham is setting up equipment. His mop of brown hair is messier than usual, and I watch him brush it out of his eyes several times. His clothes are entirely retro: flannel shirt, torn jeans. After a few minutes he notices me watching him and runs over.

He has a huge smile on his face. "Hey, you made it."

His good mood is infectious and I find myself grinning back. The vague feeling of discomfort I expect to feel isn't there. "Of course. I've had to wait weeks to hear Happy Hunting Grounds, since someone never gave me a CD."

He laughs. "Hold on. I think I know a way to fix that," he says, then darts off to a table in the back near a blue-haired girl taping a poster to the wall. The poster, like the three T-shirts hanging beside it, has the Happy Hunting Grounds logo, an intertwined HHG.

Graham hands me a CD. It's called *Greener Pastures* and has a picture of a meadow at sunset. I flip it over and see him and his bandmates standing by a stream. Nobody is looking at the camera. "There you go," he says. "No more complaining."

"I'm impressed with the merch. CDs and posters are one thing, but T-shirts." I shake my head. "Very world-tour."

He leans against a bar stool. "Don't be. We only have the three. Tony's mom makes them herself and she's a really slow supplier."

"Oh, so if I buy one," I say, my eye on the cute baby tee in emerald green, "I'll be draining your stock by a full thirty-three percent?"

"Absolutely," he agrees quickly, "but don't let that stop you."

I take a sip of beer and run through a few calculations in my head. The shirt is only fifteen dollars. With allowance due on Sunday, I could totally swing that. "All right. As soon as Lily gets here we'll go take a look. It's been weeks since we've been shopping together."

"Hey, Lily's not coming. Didn't she call you?"

I pull my phone out of my purse and check the display. Wouldn't you know it: one message. "There she is. She must have called when I was on the subway. That's a bummer. What happened?"

Graham rests his elbows on the bar. "Her mom."

This is the last thing I expect him to say. "Her mom?"

"Yeah, Vivienne got weepy."

I stare at him, dumbfounded. The Carmichaels don't cry—not Lily, not her father, most certainly not her mother. Vivienne has only two speeds: excessively cheery or excessively bitter. Everything in between simply doesn't exist. When Lily got hit in the head with a baseball in third grade and was rushed to the emergency room with a concussion, all Vivienne did was stalk up and down the hospital corridor, listing people she was going to sue: the batter, the coach, the Little League association, the town, the baseball manufacturer. "I don't understand."

"I don't think Lily does, either. All I know is that Vivienne complained that she doesn't spend enough time with her daughter, and when Lily said she spends too much time with her daughter, thank you very much, Vivienne started to cry. Lily was horrified. Her mom's makeup ran everywhere. I'm sure she explains it all on the message. I've gotta finish setting up so you should probably call her," he says, straightening. "But don't forget to buy the tee. No telling when Mrs. B will get around to making another."

I dial Lily, baffled by what's going on. It's so weird.

She answers on the third ring. "Save me," she says as soon as she picks up. "I'm being tortured."

Her voice is so low I can barely hear her. "What?"

"We're getting pedicures," she explains in a whisper. But of course this doesn't explain anything

"Huh?"

"Mother-daughter pedicures. We're sitting side-by-side and making girl talk. She's asking me about guys. It's agonizing. Call my congressman or Amnesty or someone. Anyone. I don't care. Just get me out of here," she pleads, her voice rising to dangerously high levels. I can almost hear her clearly. "Please."

"I don't understand what's going on. Graham said your mom was crying."

"She pulled a Tammy Faye."

"Huh?

"Total mascara mudslide," she says. "I found the incriminating wet n wild in her handbag. I knew something was up. The fancy stuff she uses wouldn't run in a typhoon."

I try to imagine the chic and elegant Vivienne Carmichael in a drugstore buying a cheap tube of mascara, but I simply can't do it. She's far too conscious of her status in the community to run the risk. Then I add dark sunglasses, a Burberry trench coat, and a Hermès scarf, and it becomes a little easier. Still, I try to be fair. "But she was crying, so maybe she's really upset about something. It's possible, right?"

"There are onions in the fridge," she says.

"What?" I ask, shocked. Other than condiments, the only things in Lily's fridge are bottles of Cristal and Zone meals.

"She bought apples to make it look good but I'm not fooled. I don't know what she hopes to gain by doing this but it can't— Oh, shit, she's just realized I'm on the phone." Although I can't make out any of the words, I hear the rumble of a high-pitched conversation as mother and daughter talk to each other. After almost a minute Lily comes back on the line. "I've got to go," she says in a whisper so soft I have to cover my other ear to hear her. "Vivienne wants to know if I'm talking to a boy. I've just made up an older French boyfriend to torment her. Call you tomorrow." Then she giggles loudly and speaks in a perfectly normal tone. "*Bisous* to you, too, Pierre."

Having no idea what to think, I put my phone away and stare at my Corona. Although it seems to me totally possible that Vivienne is feeling lonely and simply wants the company of her daughter, Lily's suspicions make sense. Vivienne is usually too busy for typical mother-daughter bonding rituals like pedicures and prom-dress shopping and chatting about boys (or anything, for that matter). As a board member for several local organizations, she's continually on the go, either planning gala fund-raising dinners or attending them.

Still, she *is* about to get a divorce and who knows what kind of funny things that does to a person. It has to be scary for someone her age to be single again. I mean, forty-something men are no prize. They're all bald and pudgy and smell like coffee or tobacco. And she's not exactly young and beautiful anymore. Sure, she still has a nice figure (thank you, Zone), but the crows'-feet around her eyes are fierce. Sometimes she even has that freakish, shiny, crinkle-free Botox forehead, which is much worse than wrinkles.

"So you got the full scoop?" Graham says, sliding onto the stool next to mine.

Onstage, a fellow Happy Hunting Grounder in flannel is standing at the mic singing "Take Me Out to the Ball Game" over and over again. Either he's checking sound levels or warming up his voice.

"Yeah. I got the scoop, although I can't say it was full. Something's definitely missing."

"Now you sound like Lily."

I shrug. It doesn't seem right to bad-mouth Vivienne to Graham. If Lily wants him to know all about her insane family, she'll tell him.

"I know I don't have all the facts," he says quietly. I have to lean in closer to hear him over the a cappella singing. "But I know things are crazy for Lily right now. She tries to shrug it off like nothing's wrong. She even makes jokes about it. But it's getting her down. I can tell. She's really fragile right now. She needs all the support she can get."

I open my mouth to defend myself because whether or

not he means it to, this little speech sounds like an attack on me. I'm Lily's support network. I'm her first line of defense. I'm the one who has her back and I don't need some guy she just met telling me how to be her friend.

But before I can say anything, he's holding up a hand and shaking his head. "Hey, I know you know this. You two are as close as sisters. I just needed to say it because I'm worried about her. I haven't known her long but I care."

The anger sweeps out of me at this simple statement. Of course he's worried about her. Of course he cares. He's her boyfriend. This time, for the first time, Lily got herself a really sweet one. Too bad she won't keep him.

"I just thought, you know, since you go way back, you could keep an extra-special eye on her. I know it's a really busy summer for you. Lily's always talking about what article you're working on now or what party you went to the night before. But I just thought it's something you could keep in mind."

Before I can respond the microphone screeches loudly and Graham stands up. "That's my cue. I'll see you after the set, right?"

"Absolutely," I say with an emphatic nod.

Once he's gone I stare at the Corona label and think about what he said. Is Lily fragile? I can't say. I haven't seen enough of her in the last few weeks to know. We've chatted on the phone a lot, but that's not the same. For one thing, our conversations tend to be quick and functional: Set up a date, break a date, dissect Michael Davies's latest gift. For another, Lily is hard to read. She's very self-contained and rarely complains about anything, even this divorce. She prefers to focus on the positive, like her car or the apartment she's trying with little success to finagle. The only way to know what she's really thinking is to look her in the eye.

So: I need to spend more time with Lily.

Coming up with the solution is easy. Implementing it is hard. As Graham said, I have a lot going on right now. The internship is crazy busy. The second I finish one thing, Adele dumps another six on me. The Savvy Girl deadline is fast approaching and requires all my spare time. I'd love to go shopping with Lily tomorrow but I have to be mature and responsible. Besides, it's not like the wedding is going to happen tomorrow. It's in three weeks.

I could skip Jessica's party tomorrow night and hang out with Lily instead. The mall doesn't close until ten on Saturdays, so we'd be able to hit a lot of stores.

But even as I consider the option, I know I won't do it. Jessica's party is one of those once-in-a-lifetime opportunities she was talking about. When else will I get to hang with a famous editor and her real-life friends? A work party is neat but it's almost predetermined. I mean, you have to work with the people you work with (unless you're the boss—then you can fire the people you can't stand). But a birthday party is a special occasion. You invite only the people you like. Like me.

I *have* to go.

Maybe if I work diligently on Saturday, I can do something with Lily on Sunday. Sure, finishing the second draft would be nice but not necessary. Lois would never know the difference.

I'm still trying to figure out the weekend and Lily when Happy Hunting Grounds takes the stage. A surprisingly large group of fans swarms the stage, blocking my view of Graham. Beer in hand, I shoulder my way to the front. Graham is to the left, playing guitar with so much focus he seems hardly aware that there's a cheering crowd. I find this intense concentration fascinating, and it's hard to take my eyes off him.

Listening, I get a sense for the first time of what grunge infusion is and decide after a while that a better description is grunge lite. The guitars are heavy but not overwhelming, and the lyrics are just this side of understandable. The lead singer is mumbling and swallowing his words like any self-respecting grunge rocker, but he's nowhere near the totally unintelligible mutter of Kurt Cobain.

They play a fifty-minute set, with four encores, the last of which seems to be a real one, as the band has nothing prepared and does a messy cover of "Smells Like Teen Spirit."

After helping the band load the van Graham sits at the bar with me and asks about my internship. I tell him all about Adele and Savvy Girl and going to a party at a $70 million apartment atop the Pierre hotel. Then he tells me about his famous-in-music-circles parents and songwriting and his hopes for Juilliard.

The conversation is so easy, so effortless, so natural, I have no idea time is passing. One moment Graham is thanking everyone for coming out and the next it's a little after eleven. Panicked, I call my mom to tell her I'll be late. She's huffy about the belated notice but cool.

Graham and I catch the E train uptown, talking the entire way. When we get to Penn Station, I still have ten minutes before my train, so Graham offers to buy me an ice-cream cone. "Unless you prefer a doughnut," he adds.

"Ha-ha," I say, blushing.

They announce my train, and although I assure him that this time I can find the platform on my own, he insists on going with me. He even follows me onto the train.

"But you're not going to Bellmore," I say, unable to explain why this observation makes me sad.

"No, but I've been wanting to do this for a long time."

I pick a two-seater, put down my bag, and turn to him. "Do what?"

His eyes are so alight with humor, I know he's going to say some outrageous thing that will make me blush even more. I try to look away, but he's staring at me with such quiet intensity, I feel compelled to stare back. It's like he's onstage again, extremely focused, and suddenly I have that awful thought: *I'll take a kiss.*

Appalled, I turn away, the guilt so overwhelming I can barely breathe. How could I even think that? Lily's my best friend. I'd *never* do anything to hurt her. It doesn't make sense. I don't even like Graham. I'm in love with Michael Davies.

It's the atmosphere, I think. It's the weird way fluorescent lighting makes his eyes sparkle like diamonds.

I'm so embarrassed, I don't know where to look. I focus on a red ponytail just over his shoulder and repeat the question: "Do what?"

If Graham notices my sudden awkwardness, he doesn't let on. "Put you on a train and watch you stay there."

"Ha-ha. You're *very* funny," I say with sarcasm, but it's only halfhearted. The thing is, Graham *is* very funny. He makes me laugh and he's easy to talk to and I like being around him.

"That's what they tell me," he says as the conductor announces the last call for the train to Babylon. The doors will be closing in a minute. "So we're good? I go, you stay?" I roll my eyes instead of answering and he smiles. "I'll take that as a yes."

Then he gives me one last uncertain look, as if I'm really going to follow him to the door even though I'm stone-cold sober (and don't get me wrong: I do think about following), and turns to go. I watch him walk down the aisle, onto the platform, and up the stairs to the concourse level, suddenly more confused than I've ever been in my life.

The ABCs
of the
A-List

The hunt for the perfect Jessica Cordero birthday present eats up most of Saturday morning. I spend an hour at Borders, torn between *Pride and Prejudice* and *The Fountainhead*. The former is one of my all-time favorite books but the latter seems, by all reports (I've yet to read it), more weighty and important. In the end I give up on the novel idea entirely and buy her a Zagat's restaurant guide. I'm pretty sure she has one already so I get a gift receipt. It's the thought that counts.

When I get home, I call Lily. Her voice mail picks up again. I haven't spoken to her since last night in the bar. At nine this morning she left a message telling me to call Human Rights Watch immediately and report that Vivienne is making her go to some spa in Manhasset for a mother-daughter mud bath. "Do you understand what that means? My mother will be naked. Across from me. In mud. Doesn't that violate the Geneva Convention?"

"Hey, Lil, it's me," I say, annoyed to be leaving a message. I want to talk to her to make sure she's all right. "Sounds like our shopping plans have been postponed, which is perfect for me. I've got to stay in all weekend until I get this Savvy Girl thing done. My boss is expecting it first thing Monday."

At one o'clock I sit down at my computer and begin writing my column. Because I don't know what I want to say exactly, coming up with the first line is impossible. I stop and change tactics. Instead of forcing my mind to go where it's not ready to, I sit on my bed and write down all the ideas I want to include. I take out my research and reread it, high-lighting all the pertinent facts. Five hours later, I have a co-herent list of subjects, terms, and definitions.

Feeling satisfied with a good day's work, I hop into the shower. The hardest part of any project is figuring out the pertinent info and arranging it in a useful order. I've done that. Now all I have to do is wake up tomorrow and write the story. With everything so perfectly organized—on paper and in my head—the first line will come effortlessly. Just in case it doesn't, I resolve to think about it on the train.

When I get to Mariposa, there's already a line out front. It's pretty early for the New York scene but the club is the hottest spot in the city and impossible to get into. It's owned by an Italian race car driver and has a supersecret

VIP lounge somewhere in the back where all the celebs hang out—or so Citysearch says.

Most places in Manhattan don't charge a cover before eleven P.M., but Mariposa is so hip, it always costs twenty bucks to get in, even at a total-loser hour like eight o'clock.

The line moves incredibly slowly. After twenty minutes I've barely crawled an inch. Not a single person has been let in. Bored, I check my phone for messages.

"Hey," Jessica says, tapping me on the shoulder.

I look up, surprised that the birthday girl isn't already inside. She has three people with her, one of whom looks vaguely familiar. It takes me a second to realize it's Simone Peterson, the photo editor. She's wearing *a lot* more makeup now than she does in the office. "Oh, hi."

"What are you doing in line?" Jessica asks.

The girl in front of me takes two whole steps forward. I follow. Now we're getting somewhere. "Waiting," I explain, even though it's obvious.

Jessica laughs. "That's adorable."

A blush creeps over my cheeks as I try to figure out what I've done wrong.

Seeing my confusion, she adds, "We don't wait in line. I know the manager. We're on the list. Come on." She tugs my hand.

My heart pounds with excitement after hearing the four most beautiful words in the English language: *We're on the list.* It's so incredibly exciting. Even though I had nothing to do with getting us on the list, it still feels like a stunning personal achievement. Life is about who you know, and for the first time ever I know the right people. (So really I *have* achieved something.)

Amazingly, being on the list is even better than I imagined. Not only do we not have to wait, we don't have to pay or show ID, either. We simply breeze by the bouncer, who waves us in while keeping one eye trained on the huddled masses, who yell things like "Hey, who are they?" as we walk past.

Who are we? I think as I follow Jessica into the club. *We are the people you've always wanted to be.*

Jessica's friends have staked out a quiet corner of olive velvet banquettes in a dark curtained room near the front. I slide in next to Simone because she's a familiar face while Jessica introduces me to everyone. There are too many names to keep straight—I'll admit I'm a *little* nervous to be surrounded by so many glamorous strangers—but quite a few of the group turn out to be fellow *Savvy*-ites. The beauty editor sits next to me and begins talking to Simone about people from work. Aside from Jessica and themselves, they don't seem to like anybody, even Georgie. The art director is a fascist, the publicist is a letch, the features editor can't get anyone more famous for the cover than *American Idol* runners-up, and Margot, the accessories associate, practically runs a boutique out of the fashion closet, selling items to friends then reporting them missing to the maker. At one point they start complaining about the high school interns and how they're always underfoot, and I wait with a pounding heart to hear them say my name. But the only one they mention is Hallie. She's too eager, they say, rolling their eyes. She brings coffee by every morning whether they want it or not.

I listen as they talk over and through me for forty-five minutes, a little bored but mostly fascinated by this insiders' take. I thought there was nothing to complain about at *Savvy*. It's the perfect place to work. But apparently I'm wrong.

When the conversation turns to Adele, I lean forward and do my impersonation: "How many times do I have to say no puff pastry? If I wanted beef turnovers, I'd get the value pack at Costco."

First they're amazed—I don't think they realized anyone was sitting there between them—then impressed. Simone laughs and insists that I do another one. Luckily Adele provides a generous supply of material, and pretty soon the entire table is clapping and shouting, "Encore," even those who don't work at *Savvy*.

Flush from my success, I order another dirty martini when the waitress comes by. I don't really like the taste of them—the olive juice doesn't do much to disguise the rubbing-alcohol flavor of vodka—but it's what the senior editors are having and I want to blend in. (Only high school students and sorority girls from Hofstra order rum and Coke.) For some reason they seem to like me, and I can't wait until Monday when Hallie sees me being buddy-buddy with her boss. It won't make up for the Dalai Lama, but it feels darn good.

Jessica drops by our table and I give her my present.

"What is it with you people?" she asks, laughing as she adds my unnecessary gift to the growing pile. There are at least a dozen. Thank god I ignored her.

"I don't want a thank-you note," I explain in a hurry. "Not even a thank-you e-mail. Not even a little happy, thank-you brainwave vibe. It's a totally thank-you-free gift, I swear. Seriously, it's so small it doesn't even deserve it."

I know I sound stupid because I can hear myself rambling but Jessica doesn't notice. She wraps me in a hug, her perfume, a nice, spicy scent, enveloping me. "You are so sweet. Just for that you'll receive the only handwritten card this year."

Embarrassed, I tell her it's not necessary. She tells me it is. The more I insist that it's not, the more she insists that it is. It takes me a while to realize we're both drunk, which is why we're playing this endless insisting game. Finally I agree to receive a thank-you note from her. She hugs me again, thanks me for coming, and calls me her substitute Josie. I take it as the compliment it—I *think*—is meant to be.

"You must come with me to the Alex McQueen party on Tuesday," she says, her accent suddenly thick and strong like she's the queen of England. "Josie was supposed to go with me before the count and his château interfered. And the Dior event on Thursday. Frightfully posh. Red carpet and everything. Do say you'll come. The food will be sublime."

Before she's even done issuing the invitation, I'm nodding my head emphatically. Perhaps a little too emphatically as I instantly begin to feel dizzy and have to sit down. Jessica moves on to the next table as the waitress brings another round of dirty martinis. I have no recollection of ordering one but I'm happy to drink it. By now my taste buds are numb and I can barely taste anything.

I can't say exactly how many dirty martinis I have because after the third everything starts to run together. The number of people in our banquette changes constantly but somehow the names and faces stay the same. Everyone is interesting and funny and clever and every so often I have to remind myself this is real. I am here.

After a while we leave our booth and head to the dance floor. The music is loud and pulsating, and we dance for hours, feeling fabulously free and lighthearted. If my shoes pinch, I don't notice, and when they put me in a cab for Penn Station, I don't notice that, either. I just find myself standing on track 21 waiting for the train, which drops me at Bellmore much faster than it ever has before. Then somehow it's four in the morning and I'm letting myself into the house, where Mom is sitting at the kitchen table with an *irate* look on her face, and I'm giggling every time she says "irresponsible." Everything after that is blurry.

I'm still not sure what happened to Sunday.

Aspirin:

THE NEW
MUST-HAVE
ACCESSORY
OF THE SEASON

The world's worst hangover bleeds into Monday. I don't even remember that I'm supposed to turn in my first draft of Savvy Girl until Lois walks by my desk at noon. The second I see her, my stomach drops with gut-wrenching panic and I struggle to come up with a good excuse for why I haven't done my homework.

But it's not necessary. Lois is so busy, she doesn't even say hello.

Knowing I've somehow dodged a bullet, I utterly and completely resolve to write draft one today. As soon as I get home. As soon as I leave the building. As soon as my head stops pounding.

While I'm waiting for this momentous event, I do whatever Adele tells me at a snail's pace, feeling definitely, absolutely, positively, without question certain I'll never have another drink again. Only beer from now on. Beer and, like, wine coolers for the rest of my life. I swear.

I'm so wiped out that I don't even bat an eyelash when Michael Davies materializes at my desk. I've been waiting for this moment forever and all I can do is smile weakly (at least I hope I'm smiling—my lips are still a little numb). He's as gorgeous as ever in his gray pinstripe suit and bright blue tie, and although I want to be intimidated by his perfection, I simply don't have the energy.

"Hey," he says as Adele drops another stack of query letters on my desk. She looks him up and down, then walks away with a frown. I don't know what her problem is. Seriously: Everything annoys her.

He leans against the side of my cubicle. "You look beat. Tough weekend?"

I know I'm nowhere near 100 percent, but nor do I think I'm wearing my hangover on my sleeve. My top is brightly colored to make me seem vivacious and alert, and the blue eye shadow on my lids is supposed to perk up my pale, tired complexion. Obviously I'm deluding myself.

Despite my exhaustion I suddenly have enough energy to feel self-conscious. I run a hand over my hair, which is pulled back neatly in a clip.

"No. I just..." I can't own up to being such a lightweight that I'm hungover from a night on the town *two days ago*. "I just have a cold." I cough. It's a pathetic sound but that only makes my story more believable.

He glances at my filing cabinet, where the tulips are

holding on for dear life. I threw out two stems this morning because their tips were brown and crumbly. "The flowers still look good."

"I know. I thought I'd lose them over the weekend but they're a hearty bunch. Thanks again."

He shrugs. "No problem. I saw them on the street and thought of you."

Oh, no. Now I have enough energy to blush. I can't believe he's just admitted that random things remind him of me. Like I'm on his mind to begin with. It's amazing. I don't know where we go from here. Does he ask me out? Do I ask him out? Do I play it cool like it doesn't matter to me either way? I have no idea. I should have written a script, something with cues to tell me how to behave. At the very least I should have run through possible scenarios.

As if sensing my discomfort, he says, "Are you doing anything tonight? Do you want to hang out?"

Do I? Yes, yes, yes, please, I think in a giddy rush. I've been waiting for this to happen for weeks, and now that it has, I can't even form a complete thought. Just: *Yes, yes, yes, please.*

Luckily I'm the perfect amount of exhausted to seem cool and composed. "That sounds great. Sure." Images flit through my head of us walking hand-in-hand along the Hudson River while we talk about all the important moments in our life. Maybe we'll stop to watch the students at the trapeze school soar from swing to swing. Maybe we'll both say, at the exact same time, "Hey, I've always

190

wanted to try that." And then maybe we'll kiss as the sun slips behind Jersey City. It's all too beautiful for words.

The lovely future is so consuming that I tune out the present for a second. When I tune in again, Michael is apologizing for a scheduling snafu. Uh-oh. I've missed something important.

"I forgot I'm on deadline," he continues. "What about tomorrow?"

My disappointment—which is *keen*—is tempered by the fact that I'm on deadline tonight, too, a fact that slipped my mind as well. I can't put off the SG column a moment longer. Lois is sure to remember it tomorrow.

"Tuesday's out," I say with genuine regret. "I have a party right after work. What about the next day?"

He shakes his head. Wednesday's no good, either. "What's this party?"

I close my eyes for a second. The details are a bit hazy. "Book launch in the meatpacking district. Some hotel."

Michael whistles, impressed. "Gansevoort. Swank."

Although I'm not entirely sure he's still speaking English, I agree. "It's a bio of Alexander McQueen. He's supposed to make an appearance."

"Sounds like a fun time," he says. "Why don't we get together after? I'll be here slaving away for the man. You can give me a call when it's over and I'll come down to meet you."

I'm about to consent to this plan when I realize how silly it is. Why should Michael have to slave away while I eat canapés with Alexander McQueen? "Hey, you should just come along," I say, my heart curiously steady as I issue the invitation. I know it's entirely wrong and that I'm lucky to have scraped through last time, but I also know how easy it is to add a name to the guest list.

His eyes light up at the offer but he plays it cool. "I should probably stay here and work but my going really does make more sense. So, yeah, count me in."

I smile, delighted. My head hurts only a little bit now. "Great. I'll put you on the list."

"Cool. I've, uh, gotta run. That stack of research for the lazy or stupid, not sure which, West Coast editor won't do itself."

He leaves with a wave and I watch him stroll away (he has such a nice stride, long and even steps). When he's completely out of view, I do the chair happy dance. Life could not get any better than this.

But then the jarring motion causes my brain to swish back and forth in my skull like a cruise ship in the middle of a storm, and I realize a few life improvements could stand to be made.

"You didn't take aspirin," Jessica says accusingly. Surprised, I look up and find her standing over me with an amused expression. "I told you several times to take two aspirin before you go to bed. It's the only surefire way to avoid a hangover."

I don't have any recollection of this advice. The last thing I remember her telling me was to put my legs into the cab so she could shut the door. But even if she did say something about aspirin, it wouldn't have made a difference. I was so gone on Saturday night I could barely find my bed, which hasn't moved in fifteen years, so I doubt I'd have been able to locate a small bottle of pills that migrates from one cabinet to another.

"Poor baby," she says sympathetically, patting me on the head like I'm a small child who bruised her knee. "I've got aspirin in my office if you want to try some damage control now. They're little white miracle workers."

Since I'm willing to try anything, I follow her to her office. On the way we talk about Saturday night. She tells me how much her friends liked me and I tell her how much I liked her friends. Already the staff is treating me differently. Simone and I shared an elevator this morning and collectively moaned about our hangovers. It was the neatest thing ever.

Jiggling the two aspirin in my left hand, I pick up the invite for the *McQueen of England* party. It's a glossy postcard with the silhouette of a man wearing a crown. "Is this the book's cover?"

"Yeah. A little dull. It could use some color, maybe a few rhinestones."

I flip it over to read the RSVP info and see to my delight that it's Olivia Cornersmith again. If I have any doubts that adding Michael's name is the right thing to do, the publicist's name puts them to rest. Clearly this is meant to be.

Back at my desk I dial Olivia's number and silently cheer when Elton answers the phone. This is way too easy.

"Elton darling," I say, confidently launching into my adopted persona, "it's Jessica Cordero. How are you?"

"Jessie, sweetie, so lovely of you to call. I'm devastated that we didn't get to chat at the Stella fete. I kept trying to get near you but the needy vultures from the weeklies kept getting in my way."

"Darling, you don't have to explain," I say kindly. I like forgiving Elton Valley. It makes me feel very important. "I was there. I saw what a madhouse it was."

"But a divine madhouse, no?"

"Oh yes, *such* a divine madhouse," I agree shamelessly. "I'm afraid, darling, that I've been naughty again. I have to add another name to the list for the *McQueen of England* party. It's the same as before, Michael Davies. He's the nephew of my publisher. You know how it is with these big muckety-mucks. One has to do whatever they say."

"Jessica, sweetheart, no apology necessary. If anyone understands the tyranny of the muckety-muck, *c'est moi.* I'm adding his name right now. That was the old-fashioned spelling of Davies, right? D-a-v-i-e-s."

"Aren't you the loveliest love on the planet earth?" I ask, realizing as I do that I'm getting a little carried away. It's one thing to say "muckety-muck" without raising any eyebrows; "loveliest love" pretty much crosses the line.

"Now you're just trying to embarrass me," Elton coos.

Impossible, I think. *Nobody who says* c'est moi *in a casual phone conversation is capable of embarrassment.*

"I have to go, sweetie," he adds. "The other line is ringing. One of those dreaded muckety-mucks calling to tyrannize over me. But I'll see you at the McQueen fete, right? We have so much to catch up on."

Not at all worried this time about his threat to see me at the party (thank god for weekly vultures, whatever they are), I hang up, feeling very satisfied with myself. Not only is Michael in, my headache has started to fade.

GET YOUR
BUTS
IN GEAR:
*Useful Excuses
to Have on Hand*

I devote Monday night entirely to Savvy Girl. I say hello to my parents, who are still pissed at me for coming home at four in the morning stumbling drunk without a call (Mom left *five* messages on my cell, each one more angry than the last), and disappear into my room. I don't even take the time to eat dinner. My only concern is my essay. I need a first sentence and I need it fast.

I work on it for an hour before I throw my notebook across the room in frustration. Everything I come up with sounds stiff and formal, like the intro to a long, boring investigative piece for *Harper's*. My opening sentence needs to have pizzazz. It has to grab the reader by the throat and not let go.

Tired but not discouraged, I jump right into the second paragraph. (Who needs a first sentence, anyway?) By now

I know two things for sure: what I want to do with my column and what I want my column to do. If I can make people aware of the restrictions to their personal liberties, then they can take steps to protect those freedoms.

Pulling that off is the challenge, but at midnight I print out what I have to show Lois in the morning. It's not a complete first draft, but at more than half it gives the reader a good idea of where I'm going.

Exhausted but satisfied, I fall into bed, not at all worried about the elusive first line. It'll come to me when it's ready.

I wake with this optimistic thought still in mind, dress quickly, and run downstairs to breakfast. I'm suddenly starving.

My parents are already in the kitchen. My dad is finishing a slice of toast while reading the *Times*. Mom is mixing instant oatmeal. I pour a cup of coffee as my stomach growls again.

"Can I have some of that?" I ask Mom, who's usually dying to give away oatmeal. She hands me a packet and tells me to make it myself. She doesn't even smile. "Yeesh. I *said* I was sorry."

Neither parent responds, which is fine with me. I don't need to rehash old business during breakfast, either.

We eat in relative silence, with NPR in the background. As usual, I tune it out, instead thinking about my date with Michael later. I try to imagine what the Gansevoort Hotel is like. Hopefully it will have lots of quiet loungey corners where two people can sit and really get to know each other. I come up with several topics of conversation to have on hand: his internship, my internship, his college experience, his family, his hometown, his hobbies, his favorite movies, his favorite books.

When I finish my oatmeal, I put the bowl in the dishwasher (a shameless play for parental forgiveness), kiss Mom on the cheek, and say good-bye. Then I remind her that I'm going to be late. "I have an event," I say, my hand on the doorknob. Dad is already in the car.

Mom shakes her head. "No, you don't."

I stop and check the day: This *is* Tuesday. "Yes, I do. It's a work thing. I have to go."

But Mom is adamant. "The only thing you have to do is be here by seven."

Amazed, I stare at her. This is totally unbelievable. I've never been grounded in my entire life. "You can't be serious," I say, *overcome* with outrage. Troubled kids, shoplifters, B students get grounded. Not me. Certainly not for a first offense. "But that's insane. And completely unfair. I don't deserve that."

"I am serious," Mom says in a deadly calm voice that says the case is closed. "You broke the rules, and there are consequences. We'll discuss for how long when you get home tonight."

"But this is the first time I've ever done anything wrong," I say, my voice dangerously close to a screech. "The very first time! It's not fair to punish me for one mistake.

And, besides, I have a work thing. It'll probably be dull and boring. But it's work."

Mom stares at me blankly, and I realize I'm not getting anywhere. I switch tactics. Anger, although completely justified, won't sway my mother. At the moment she's too full of parental righteousness to be bullied. And with good cause. I should have called. If I hadn't been so drunk, I totally would have.

Raising your parents is tricky business, and sometimes—like now, when you want to be ungrounded, or later, when you put them in a nursing home—you have to be up-front and honest with them in order to do it right. It's not always easy because they don't want to hear the truth, but it's necessary for their own good.

I look up and meet her gaze head-on. Eye contact is very important for a heart-to-heart. "I know where you're coming from, Mom, and I understand why you're worried. I'd be angry, too, if the situations were reversed. But the thing you have to remember is I'm a good kid. I'm smart. I can think for myself and make the right decisions. I don't smoke. I don't take drugs. I don't randomly hook up with guys. I'm responsible. You *have* to trust me," I say, uncomfortably aware that teens in my position have been saying the same words for the last two thousand years. I need something more. I pause for a moment to think, then it hits me in a burst of inspiration. Seriously: What I come up with is so brilliant, it should be posted on a teen site for how to deal with your parents. "More than that, Mom, you have to trust yourself to have raised me right."

Mom listens intently and nods. Although she's still angry with me, she's open to reason. Quietly and in that same deadly calm voice, she asks me how she can trust me when I came home at four in the morning too drunk to stand.

My first impulse is to point out that I *could* stand. Walking was a problem, absolutely, but standing in place was totally doable. But I recognize that getting defensive won't help my maturity argument, so I agree with her completely. "Saturday is a perfect example of what I'm talking about. I had too much to drink, yes, and was, as you saw, extremely drunk. But I learned something from it. I now know that four drinks"—since I can't remember how many I had, this isn't exactly a lie—"are too many for me. I won't ever do that again. Isn't that what being a teenager is all about? Identifying boundaries? Recognizing mistakes? It's a learning curve. In a weird way Saturday was a good thing. It taught me a huge lesson about alcohol, one that I'll never forget. I'm never going to figure this stuff out if you don't let me."

Although my mom has a pretty good bullshit radar, I can tell that she's being swayed. I go in for the kill. "Next year I'll be away at college, on my own, doing who knows what. Won't you feel better knowing you don't have to worry about me?"

She smiles wryly. "No matter what you do, I'll worry."

God, sometimes she's *such* a parent. "Okay. But maybe you'll worry a little less."

To my surprise, Mom nods slowly and thinks about what I've said. I wait patiently, which isn't easy. Part of me wants to keep making my case until I get a resounding yes, but I know better than to push. Either a gentle shove works or it doesn't. There's no in-between.

Outside, in the driveway, Dad honks his horn. We're already late for the 8:12.

"All right," Mom says finally, "but only because it's work-related. The grounding resumes Friday at six o'clock P.M. and will last two weeks. You will keep your phone on and answer whenever it rings. We will be doing spot checks, so you'd better be sober and lucid. If I hear so much as one giggle, your father and I will be there to drag you home so fast your head will spin, and we don't care if we embarrass you in front of your colleagues."

Although I want to jump up and cheer triumphantly (the "trust yourself" line had to be the clincher), I take the mature-behind-my-years route and thank her with an emphatic promise that she won't regret her decision. Then I run out to the car before she changes her mind.

On the way to the station I have to have the conversation all over again with my dad. He's a marshmallow compared with Mom and compliments me on my maturity. Parents—they're a piece of cake.

Once in the office I take out my SG piece to read through one last time before giving it to Lois. I'm mostly looking for typos and weird breaks in logic but by the end of the second page, I'm too embarrassed to hand it in to anyone, let alone Lois, who thinks I'd make an excellent Savvy Girl correspondent. The insightful paragraphs about inalienable rights I wrote late last night aren't nearly as profound in the bright light of day (or make as much sense). My column reads like a boring social studies paper. I have too much history and not enough commentary. It's supposed to be written from the perspective of a seventeen-year-old girl but I'm nowhere in the story. Somehow I left myself out.

Discouraged, I call Lily to cheer me up. I haven't told her yet about my date with Michael and she hasn't filled me in on the mother-daughter spa day. It feels like ages since we've spoken.

"Hey, chica," I say as soon as she picks up the phone. "Guess who I'm going out with tonight?"

I don't even need to say his name. "Congratulations. That's great." She's got the words down but the enthusiasm is missing.

"You still think he's up to something, don't you?" I ask suspiciously. I'm disappointed with her reaction. I want her to be 100 percent happy for me like I am for myself.

"No," she says. "I'm sure he's totally into you." Again, her tone is perfunctory and uninterested.

"Hey, what's up?" I ask, wondering what her parents did now. Man, they are such losers.

"Nothing."

"You can't fool me," I say. "Come on, give. What'd they do?"

"What who?" She does a decent job of sounding totally confused but you can't fool your best friend.

"Your parents. Seriously: Did Vivienne make you get mother-daughter bikini waxes after the mud bath?"

"No, she had a dinner party. We were home by eight." She pauses for a moment. "I called you."

My heart skips as I try to remember if I spoke to Lily while at the club. The memories are hazy but I feel certain I wouldn't have answered my phone with music and laughter blaring in the background. "You did?"

"Yeah, I called your house around ten to see if you were up for a study break but nobody answered." She pauses again. I can't remember the last time Lily sounded so serious. Even when she was mad at me over the Stella party, she retained her sense of humor. "So I *might* be wondering what happened to you."

I know—unquestionably, without a doubt—that Lily would understand my going into the city for Jessica's birthday (see: "the fabulous imperative") but there's no point in bringing it up. Even though she'd totally get it, she'd still be hurt. "My parents were out and I was asleep," I explain, fully aware that this is the first lie I've ever told her. But it's a little white one, the kind that doesn't count. "I was so wiped out from SG research I crashed at, like, eight-thirty. I'm surprised I didn't hear the phone ring. I must have been in a very deep sleep."

203

The words sound phony to my own ears. I'm over-explaining. I'm being too specific. But before Lily realizes anything's wrong, I jump in with an invite to Thursday's Dior party. "Scarlett Johansson will be there," I say in a rush. "And a red carpet. It's going to be amazing. You *have* to come."

It's a spur-of-the-moment decision but the second I say the words I realize it's the perfect solution. Graham said Lily was fragile. He said she needed my support. Now I can be there for her and give her a little taste of the fabulous imperative. Plus she might get to meet Scarlett Johansson. It's win-win-win.

"Really?" she asks hesitantly. "You sure you're allowed to bring a guest?"

What a silly question. Of course I'm not. But if I'm willing to stick my neck out for some guy I barely know (albeit a future husband), the least I can do is stick it out for my best friend. "It's fine."

"Then yes, yes, yes," she said excitedly. "Totally count me in. You're the best friend ever."

I hang up, feeling so good about my generosity that I forget about the Savvy Girl mess on my desk until I look down.

I spend the next two hours trying to spice up the text. It shouldn't be so hard: Pill equals sex; sex equals spice. While I work, I keep one eye out for Lois, prepared to either babble out an excuse or dodge her entirely. When she drops by Adele's desk to discuss an article about locker-room etiquette, I run to the bathroom and stay there for twenty minutes. By the time I return she's back in her office on the phone.

Somehow I manage to get through the day without her asking about my article.

The *McQueen of England* party is the perfect thing to take my mind off SG. For the first hour Jessica introduces me to important fashion people as her protégée. It sounds really impressive and the first time she says it, I blush. I have always wanted to have a mentor—it's what I thought Lois would be before I found out how busy she is—and feel positive that the evening couldn't get better.

Then Michael arrives. He goes straight to the bar to get a Chimay, which is the exact thing I'm drinking. (Jessica had offered me a pink Bazookatini when we first arrived, but I kept my word to my parents and stuck to beer—their trust in me is so justified.) When he returns, I point out a few isolated spots that are perfect for deep, meaningful conversation, but he shrugs and says he likes being in the thick of things.

It's louder in the thick, and I have to shout to be heard. He responds to my questions about school (GW) and his major (communications) with succinct, one-word answers. He's a man of few words, which I like. The strong, silent type is so sexy, although a *little* difficult to talk to. Sometimes, like at a cocktail party, you need an easygoing guy like Graham to chat with.

Jessica spots us from across the room and comes over

for an introduction. She winks at me when Michael flashes his killer smile. He's obviously heard of her and is as impressed as I am with the famous fashion editor's history. His face is animated as he asks her a ton of questions about life as a model: who she knows, who she likes, where she's been. Jessica is gracious and answers his questions, but after ten minutes she excuses herself to talk to the author of *McQueen of England.* Michael falls silent again before returning to the bar to get another beer. He forgets to ask if I want a refill.

The bar is really crowded and Michael disappears for ages. I feel awkward standing in the middle of the floor alone, so I go look for him. He's in the garden gazing deeply into the eyes of a skinny brunette with so much cleavage it's practically brushing her chin. Mortified, I apologize for interrupting and walk away. I feel so stupid for thinking he could like plain old me with my maybe-on-a-good-day-B cups. Before I get ten feet Michael runs after me to explain that the woman thought she'd lost her contact lens and he was trying to find it. I know it's not true but I'm too relieved he thinks I'm worth chasing to call him on it.

I stay for another hour but the sparkle has gone out of the evening. Despite Michael's sudden interest in *Savvy* and my life, all I want is to be home with my family. I take an early train and arrive in Bellmore before ten. My parents are in the den watching a gory forensic crime show. When it cuts to commercial, Mom mutes the TV and asks how the event was. I tell them it was more interesting than I expected and that I met some important people. Mom smiles and turns the sound back on. I say good night and slowly climb the stairs to my bedroom, repeating silently to myself, *It* was *a good party*. I brush my teeth, wash my face, and rub moisturizer over my always dry T-zone (*it* was *a good party*). Then I put on my pajamas and get into bed.

I turn off the lamp on the nightstand and close my eyes, not at all sure why I want to cry.

YOU CAN DO IT!
CONFIDENCE-BUILDING EXERCISES

At three o'clock on Wednesday Jessica calls me into her office, tells me to have a seat, and *shuts the door.* The second I hear it click, the blood in my head starts pounding. She knows. She has to. Sometime in the last few hours, she talked to Elton, who said something about the evil muckety-mucks (because he's an evil muckety-muck himself), to which she responded in all ignorance, "What evil muckety-mucks?" and then he said (because he's so evil he loves naming names), "You know, Michael Davies's uncle," and she said with total bafflement, "Huh?" and slowly they pieced together that the evil person who has stolen her identity is none other than her adorable protégée who re-minds her of her little sister. *Oh, god.*

Don't panic. Don't panic.

Oh, god, I'm panicking.

Say you're sorry. Jump in with an apology before she even starts. Throw yourself at her feet. Beg.

"I'm sure you know what this is about," she says calmly, sitting behind her desk. I bow my head in shame. "As soon I got my hands on it, I made a copy for you."

"I don't know what I was think—" Her words sink in. I look up. "What?"

"Hallie's Savvy Girl entry." She pushes several sheets of paper across the desk. "She turned hers in this morning, and someone leaked it. I thought you'd want to see it."

It takes me a little while to process the fact that the world isn't ending. No, it's simply that Hallie turned in her column two days early (the suck-up). "I do. That's fabulous." I flip through it, scanning sentences here and there but mostly unable to concentrate because of the recent scare. My heart is still pounding. "How is it?"

She shrugs. "Pedestrian. You can do better."

I know she's trying to build my confidence, but her compliment only makes me feel more insecure. I'm so terrified of how not better I can do that I haven't even opened my SG document yet today, even though there are only *fifty-one* hours left. The clock is ticking.

"It's totally cool if you need to bail on tomorrow." She holds up the invite to the Dior party, giving me an excellent look at the RSVP info. The number is so familiar I don't even have to see Olivia Cornersmith's name to know who it's from. "The column's much more important."

She isn't saying anything I haven't thought myself a

million times in the last six hours but instead of agreeing, I tell her I'm in good shape. This morning Lily called to say she'd found the perfect outfit for the event. "And the best part?" Lily added. "I can wear it to the stupid Vegas wedding, too. It's *that* perfect."

Her excitement was paralyzing. All I could do was say, "Great."

As soon as I return to my desk, I read Hallie's essay, which details her struggle to get along with her younger twin sisters. In simple terms she explains what it's like to be the odd woman out in your own home. Sweet and thoughtful, the story fails to address a single major issue or have a global reach. It's good, but for a Hallmark greeting card, not the most influential women's magazine in the country.

Feeling a surge of confidence and impatience, I shut down my computer. It's not even four o'clock but it's time to leave. I have to go home and work on my SG article. I totally have Hallie beat. I just have to finish mine to prove it.

I stick her article into my bag and take out the train schedule. Just as I reach for the switch on my lamp, I look up and notice Michael. He's smiling.

My heart doesn't budge. I wait for it to skip a beat but it does nothing.

"Hey," I say hesitantly. I'm not sure how we left things last night. I was totally infatuated with him when he followed me to the curb to hail a cab to Penn Station and considerably less so when I got out of the taxi in Bellmore.

"Great party," he says. "Thanks again for inviting me. It's a shame we didn't get to hang out afterward."

I nod. It is a shame. Maybe if we had, I wouldn't feel so confused and strangely indifferent now. I *want* to like him. He's everything a first serious boyfriend should be: older, experienced, smart, gorgeous.

"Should we try again tomorrow night?" he suggests.

"I've got that Dior thing, remember?" I'd mentioned it last night when he asked if I had more parties coming up. I bragged about Scarlett Johansson because it seemed like the sort of thing that would impress him. And it had.

"Oh, yeah, totally slipped my mind." When I don't respond instantly—I'm trying to figure out how truthful this statement is—he adds, "You know, if you're looking for a date, I'm totally up for it."

He makes it sound like he's doing me a favor and for a second I buy it. I'm grateful for the offer and giddy that he wants to hang out with me. But then I quickly replay the conversation in my head—no, I replay our entire history—and finally catch on. He's into the parties, not me. The charm offensive was about getting back into my good graces after dissing me for a model, an obvious tactical error. And I was stupid enough to fall for it. But seriously: What girl wouldn't love finding thoughtful little tokens on her desk every day? It was exactly what I thought a growing relationship should be.

And that should have put me on guard. Because nothing

ever works out the way it does in my dreams. If it did, Michael would be as great to talk to as Graham. And as funny. And as talented.

"So what do you think?" he asks as the silence grows. "Are we on?" Then he flashes his killer smile. Even though I see through him now, I can't help being affected by his incredible beauty. It must be amazing to go through life with a face like that.

Lily has *to see it,* I think, wondering why I'm not more hurt or angry. It's like I really don't care. Somewhere between the Gansevoort Hotel and the Bellmore station the spell wore off. That is something else Lily has to see.

"Okay," I say.

"Great. E-mail me the details. I'd stick around but I have to photocopy some articles about Seoul for the travel editor." Michael rolls his eyes. "This guy's so clueless he doesn't know where the East Side is, let alone the Far East. But you know how it is."

"No, I don't," I say, tired of his constant complaining. He makes it sound as if he's a stone being ground under the heels of incompetent tyrants. Like the editors of *Egoïste* haven't put out a successful magazine for seventeen years. "Everyone at *Savvy*'s really smart and nice and knows what they're doing. They're a pleasure to work for, so I can't relate."

Michael stares at me dumbfounded for a moment, then he grins like it's all a big joke. "Ha. Very funny. You had me going there for a minute."

As soon as he's gone, I call Elton, and in a quick, bantering conversation, pass along the dreadful news that the evil muckety-muck now has a niece as well as a nephew. He takes it in stride.

Then I flip off my lamp and dash out of the office before Adele returns from her one o'clock fitting. (Actually, she should have been back by now; this doesn't bode well for the dressmaker.) I can't wait to finish my SG essay. Ideas are running through my head as I walk to Penn Station in the staggering early-August heat. I repeat phrases three or four times in order to remember them. Once on the train I jot them down. Finally, Savvy Girl is flowing.

But as soon as I get home, as soon as I sit at my computer and try to write a coherent paragraph, the flow abruptly stops. I know what I want to say but I can't say it. The few good phrases I have stand out like sore thumbs in a sea of gibberish.

Dinnertime comes and goes but I stay glued to my desk, writing and rewriting the same dozen sentences. The right words seem only slightly beyond my grasp, as if my fingers are just skimming the bottom of the perfect paragraph. It's an incredibly frustrating feeling but oddly comforting. I know sooner or later, I'll be able to stretch high enough. I mean, what's the point otherwise?

At nine Mom, in an unprecedented display of maternal thoughtfulness, brings me a turkey sandwich and lets me eat it in my room.

At ten Dad knocks on my door and holds up two cartons

of ice cream. Chocolate chip or pistachio? I look at the nutritional labels of both and go with the one that has more sugar, hoping for an energy boost.

At eleven I delete the entire document and start from scratch.

At twelve I pick a new topic—"The Britishizing of Madonna"—and write five hundred words on why it's wrong for an American to curtsy to the queen.

At one I try to recover my deleted document from the trash. When that doesn't work, I tape together an old printed-out version and retype it into the computer.

At two I give up and go to sleep.

RACE
to the
FINISH LINE:
How to Leave a *Last*ing Impression

Although the situation is very, very desperate, I wake up Thursday morning feeling incredibly optimistic. As soon as I open my eyes, the truth hits me and I realize what the problem has been all along: no throat-pressing, do-or-die deadline. As long as I had a month or a week or even a few days, I had too much time. I'm the sort of person who needs the absolute pressure of no possible escape to get results. The worse it is, the better I do. Every paper I've ever handed in, every article I've ever written was done in the eleventh hour. I finished my *Huckleberry Finn* term paper ("Civilization Through the Eyes of Huck Finn") only ten minutes before class started, frantically scribbling the bibliography during lunch at Wendy's. I got an A plus.

I arrive at *Savvy* feeling surprisingly refreshed after only five hours of sleep. When, before I even turn on my computer, Adele drops a huge box of folders to be filed on my desk, I thank her and promise to get to it immediately.

Ignoring the folders and everything else, I start a brand-new document and begin my Savvy Girl essay one last time. The first sentence flows easily from my fingers. I write: *American women think they won the right to control their reproductive freedom long ago. Well, I'm here to tell them different.*

My second paragraph gives a short history of the Pill. The next one touches briefly on the abortion controversy. Paragraph four raises the issue of pharmacists withholding emergency contraception. I'm discussing Mississippi's "conscience clause" when Jessica stops by my desk. It's now a little after three.

"Hey, chica, I'm just dropping off those memos we talked about," she says, winking at me as she puts a manila folder into my in-box. "Be sure to take a look at those. They've got a lot of useful info." She winks again. "Call if you have questions."

Without opening the folder I know what it contains: another Savvy Girl column. The twinkle in Jessica's eye couldn't mean anything else.

As soon as she walks away, I grab the top essay, which is Lara's. Hers is no different from Hallie's. It's another confessional piece, this time about her lifelong struggle with weight. Although it's a familiar story, I read it with pangs of sympathy (and a dash of impatience). She ends on a positive note, observing that she's come to love her body for the things it can do, not the things it can wear, but I don't believe her. I've seen her munch on undressed iceberg wedges for six consecutive weeks. There's no love there.

That her essay is remarkably similar in tone and content to Hallie's should have put me at ease. If I've got one beat, then I've got the other. But instead I find myself feeling oddly agitated. There's something very appealing about their straightforward honesty. *Savvy* is about self-knowledge and growth and the struggle of each person to be a better human being. Hallie's and Lara's columns are about that struggle. Mine is about the struggle of a society over injustice. It's truth with a capital T. What if they want truth with a little T?

My heart pounding, I pick up Beth's essay, which tells the story of her eighty-five-year-old grandmother who was recently diagnosed with Alzheimer's. She goes on for several paragraphs about her family's effort to accept the awful news, but she never once manages to convey the pain she must feel visiting this cherished woman who has no idea who she is. Either Beth's a bad writer or she made the whole thing up. My money's on the latter, and I smile when I imagine poor Grandma Sophie thinking she has Alzheimer's only because she doesn't think she has Alzheimer's.

Still, despite the questionable facts, her essay is stronger than mine. It's personal and heartrending and something every person can relate to. Mine is a self-important exposé on birth control.

What was I thinking?

Very calmly, with hands steady, I put the stories back in the folder, which I stick in my top drawer. I grab my purse and walk as quickly as possible to the bathroom. I don't want to seem like I'm running, but I also don't want to start crying in the middle of the hallway. I manage to hold on long enough to close the stall door behind me. As soon as I do, the tears start streaming down my cheeks.

I know it's pathetic to cry over a dumb magazine column like some freshman girl who didn't make cheerleading but I can't help myself. Every time I think about what Savvy Girl would have meant—not just the scholarship and fame but the validation, prestige, and experience—my eyes well up. I can't put a name to it, but I know something very special has been lost.

It's so stupid. It's not like if I'd done the assignment right the editors would have picked me. No, the column would still go to Hallie for her thoughtful piece on fitting in or to Lara for her fake self-esteem. I've got nothing that compares with their pain. My life has been too easy. I'm not lucky enough to have weight problems or mean siblings who don't like me. My family is functional.

But this is no comfort. I know if I'd handed in a draft to Lois on Monday, she would have pointed me in the right direction. Then I too could have invented a sick grandmother.

The regret is so painful, I can barely breathe.

While waiting for the pitifully embarrassing tears to

stop, I think about what I'm going to do. Lois will want an explanation, as will Jessica. And probably Lisa, the executive editor. And most definitely Hallie, Lara, and Beth. I need a story, some really good reason why I couldn't be bothered to do the essay. And it has to be really, *really* good. Savvy Girl is the best thing ever to come my way.

But nothing can compete with your own column in a national consumer magazine, so I decide to say simply that I lost interest. I already have way too much going on next year and couldn't risk adding more. The only thing I have is editor of the school newspaper, but I'll throw in social chair for the prom and president of the senior class to make it look good.

By 6:15 I feel more in control. My face is still hot and my eyes are red but the hiccups have finally subsided. I wait until the bathroom is empty, then creep out of the stall to splash cool water on my face. I look like a total disaster. Everything is blotchy and swollen and I consider going back into the stall, but I decide to be brave and face it. I put on blush, eyeliner, shadow, and lipstick. The improvement is minor but enough.

My disastrous Savvy Girl article is still open on my desktop, mocking me, it seems, for my stupid optimism. Unable to bear looking at it, I toss it into the trash and immediately empty the basket. I don't ever want to see it again.

"Hey, chica," Jessica says, breezing past my cube without stopping. "Ready to leave in fifteen?"

"Absolutely," I say, smiling. It's a weak smile but mostly

sincere. The party is something to look forward to. It's at a majorly exclusive club and will be loaded with celebrities and at least one honest-to-god movie star. It's such a privilege to have been invited. I mean, no one else from the magazine is going, certainly not any of the other interns. (As far as I know, they haven't gone to a single party all summer. I really feel bad for them.)

My phone's message light is on and I call in to the voice-mail system. It's Lily saying she can't make it tonight. Something came up. I immediately call her back. She picks up after the third ring.

"What could possibly have come up?" I ask before she even says hello.

"My father. He's . . ." She trails off, breathes deeply, exhales.

Her tone is incredibly sad and so unlike Lily. "Hey, what's going on?"

"My family . . . you know my family. They suck." I can't be sure but it almost sounds like she's crying. But that's not right. Lily never cries.

"You know, I can skip this thing," I say immediately. "I can come right over and you can tell me what your sucky family has done now."

She laughs, suddenly embarrassed. "God, no. You can't miss the party because I'm a little down. It's a big deal. Scarlett Johansson, right? We can talk tomorrow. You'll be around tomorrow, right?" she asks, her tone hopeful.

Although my offer to miss the party is completely genuine, I'm hugely relieved she tells me not to. I would've done it for her because she's my best friend but I really want to go to this. I've never been to a party with real movie stars before. It seems so exciting. Maybe I'll bump into Scarlett in the bathroom and we'll start talking. Maybe she'll love *Savvy* magazine as much as Michel Dupré does. Maybe we'll become good friends and go to movie premieres together.

None of that would compensate for not being the Savvy Girl columnist or anything, but it would cheer me up.

"I'm absolutely around tomorrow," I say. "We'll get sundaes. My treat."

Lily hiccups. Oh, god. She *has* been crying. "Cookie dough?"

"What other kind is there?"

"Then I guess I'm in. Thanks."

It's on the tip of my tongue to ask one more time if she's okay—she doesn't really sound it—but Lily's my best friend. If she wants me to come out there, she'd tell me. We're always straight with each other.

She says good-bye and I hang up the phone, replaying the conversation in my head. Something about it was really off. I pick up the phone to call her back.

Then Jessica taps me on the shoulder. I jump in surprise.

"Sorry to frighten you," she says, pulling a blue silk wrap over her shoulders. She's the only person I know with a sitcom wardrobe; she never wears the same thing twice.

"You weren't responding to verbal communication. Ready to go?"

I grab my purse and follow her to the elevator. Afraid she might bring up Savvy Girl, I ask her a ton of questions about everything I can think of: apartment, friends, school. By the time we arrive at Marquee I know her entire career history dating back to her paper route in seventh grade.

The cab pulls up to the club and as soon as we open the door, a million flashes pop in my eyes. Even though nobody cares who I am, I smile and pose. I can't help it. I'm in front of the hottest club in New York City with a red carpet rolled before me and a hundred paparazzi snapping photos. I can't believe I'm here. I can't believe I might have missed this.

The red carpet is only twenty feet long and shouldn't take us more than thirty seconds to cross, but Jessica stops to chat with people. Not celebrities, other press folks, but it is still pretty amazing. I stand next to her, soaking up the experience. Seriously: What's a Savvy Girl column compared with this?

Inside Jessica makes a beeline for the bar. The club is fabulous, with a glass-beaded chandelier around a disco ball and gray banquettes and lots of purple neon (which does make it feel a *little* bit like a Long Island nightclub).

She offers me her new signature drink, a lemondrop. I'm supposed to stick to beer but feel entirely deserving of something more fun after the totally crappy day I've had.

"Cheers," she says as we clink glasses. I down mine

quickly and return it to the bar, feeling remarkably relaxed. Because I've been hanging with Jessica for a couple of weeks, a lot of faces are now familiar. Several people come over to say hello. A few even remember my name.

We're talking to a *Vanity Fair* editor when Michael Davies arrives. He sidles up next to me in his perfectly tailored beige suit, powder blue shirt, and psychedelic, pastel tie and asks if I'd like another drink. I tell him I'm good.

In fact, I'm better than good. I've already had four lemondrops and am pleasantly sloshed. Whenever I bend my head to one side, I can feel my brain sliding carelessly through my skull. It's a wonderful feeling. Nothing seems important anymore. I can think of the Savvy Girl column and what I lost and what I won't ever have without any pain. It's like it never even mattered in the first place.

And I can look at Michael and not mind his personality defects (his consuming uninterest in anything, his boredom, his constant negativity). I can see only his blue eyes; his soft, pouty lips; his tousled black hair; and his strong, chiseled jaw line with a hint of stubble. He's not nearly as interesting as he thinks he is nor as clever but what does it matter? What does any of it matter? We're at a party with a red carpet. This isn't real life. This is a fantasy, a dream I made up because my real ones won't come true.

I thread my arm through his and ask if he's seen the red room yet. He shakes his head no, so I lead him to the quiet lounge area off to the side. It's crowded but we snag a banquette near the back. Michael goes up to the bar to get drinks and I don't even mind when he spends ten minutes talking to a tall girl in a pink wig. So he has a thing for models. A lot of guys do.

I survey the crowd, looking for celebrities. There are so many beautiful, polished people it's hard to tell the some-ones from the no ones. It's almost like it's not worth the ef-fort to be famous.

Michael brings our drinks and sits down. "Cool party," he says, his eyes darting around the room.

"How are things at *Egoïste*?"

He shrugs. "You know."

"Have you done any interviews yet?"

"One. A film producer," he says. "Big know-nothing know-it-all."

He tilts his head to the side to get a better look at the bar, and I realize I've been here before. This is the boring part of being out with Michael Davies. I lean forward and, totally unself-conscious, brush my lips against his. If he's surprised by my unexpected friendliness, he doesn't show it. He puts down his drink and wraps his arms around me, and I find myself wondering, despite the press of his warm, dry lips, how often he's attacked like this.

The kiss is smooth and nice, and I wait for rockets or fireworks or even a flare gun to go off in my head. Nothing happens. I press closer, hoping to create a reaction. It doesn't work, and in part of my brain, the non-sloshing part that still winces when I remember Savvy Girl, I know that I shouldn't be thinking this much. I shouldn't be trying so hard to conjure up the image of rockets or fireworks or even a lone flare gun on a black, moonless night. This is an experiment that failed.

But the part of my brain that can see Michael's gorgeous blue eyes won't give up. It simply won't accept that a being so beautiful can leave me feeling nothing at all.

And then suddenly I feel something: Someone is pulling my shoulders back and saying, "What the hell are you doing?"

Shocked, I open my eyes and turn around and stare at him for a million long seconds before seeing who it is. And then I see him.

"Graham?" I say in a whisper. The fury in his eyes is so bright and strong, it's almost blinding, like staring directly into the sun.

"How can you do this to her?" he bites out.

His anger, palpable and fierce, scares me, and I start to shake, although I don't understand why. It's the air-conditioning, I think. Someone's turned it up to freezing.

I open my mouth to defend myself but I don't know what to say. None of it makes sense. Why is he here? Why is he yelling? Why does he hate me?

Finally, after eons or maybe just seconds, I find my voice. "Wha...what? Do what?" I ask, my eyes meeting his. But then I have to turn away. Because I can't stand the way he's looking at me: like he can't stand looking at me. How did this happen? When did this happen? Why did this happen?

"He's getting remarried. Do you understand? Re-married." He says it slowly like I'm an idiot. I don't know. Maybe I am. Maybe that's why I don't know what the hell is going on. "She's gutted and you're here making out with some pretty-boy model."

"Who's getting remarried?" Beside me the pretty-boy model stiffens. I press my hand against his shoulder. I don't care about his hurt feelings or ego. He doesn't even belong here for this. Why is he still here? Why isn't he talking to the supermodel at the bar?

"Her fucking father," Graham says with several tons of disgust.

I close my eyes as the pieces fall into place. Lily sounding weepy. Lily canceling our plans. Lily telling me to have fun without her as she hiccupped pathetically into the phone. It could be only one thing: her piece-of-shit dad marrying the slutty secretary he's been screwing for years before the ink is even dry on the divorce papers. It's just the sort of crappy thing he's been doing for all her life.

And I knew it. On the phone earlier, I knew something was hugely and seriously wrong, but I chose to ignore it. I chose not to notice. Because I didn't want to deal with it. Because I didn't want to change my plans. Because I didn't want to miss this: the hottest party of the year, my first red carpet, necking in the corner booth with the most boring, self-involved, selfish pretty-boy on the face of the earth.

I'm a piece of shit, too.

"Okay. Okay." I take a deep breath and open my eyes.

Graham is still glowering at me with his bright brown eyes, and in a flash it hits me why I've been feeling so confused lately: I like him. Graham. He's the one I want to be kissing in a dark booth. Graham.

No, it can't be Graham. I shake my head, trying to dislodge the thought. But it stays. Graham.

I struggle to focus on the important things. "I'm ready," I say. "I just need to—"

"There you are, Chrissy," Jessica says, smiling cheerfully as she pulls a suede stool up to the table. She puts down her drink, then readjusts her silk wrap. Behind her is a stubby man with a bleached-blond goatee. "I've been looking all over for you. There's someone here who wants to say hi."

My nerves are about to snap and Graham (Graham!) is glaring at me like I'm the Antichrist, so I don't notice her sly tone or the devious glint in her eye. All I see is another fashion insider who wants to make small talk. I can't deal with this now—him, her, me—but I hold out my hand and smile like there's nothing wrong. Because that's what I've learned this summer: how to fake it.

The man takes my hand in his firm grip. "Pleasure to meet you."

I'm barely looking at him but his voice gets my attention. I know that voice.

"We've spoken on the phone many times," he says,

That voice. Oh, god.

"I'm Elton Valley."

For a moment the room spins. It actually swirls and twirls around my head until it comes to rest in the place where it started: Elton Valley's coldly superior, gotcha grin.

The room is suddenly impossibly hot. I try to breathe, but the air is thick and stifling and slowly suffocating me. My limbs are completely numb. Every single part of my body has lost feeling. Except my heart. No, my heart is pounding painfully like I just ran a hundred miles.

I have to get out of here before I faint.

In a remarkably calm voice I hear myself say, "Please excuse me."

But I'm not at all calm, and as soon as I leave the room, my knees start to tremble. I climb the stairs at a snail's pace, clutching the handrail. At the door I'm forced to wait because Ms. Johansson has finally arrived. Her entourage is blocking the entrance while she talks to reporters. I try to slip past but someone clutches my arm and says, "Just a minute, ma'am." My one brush with fame.

Outside, I walk to the curb and raise my arm for a taxi. There are none in sight but I don't have the energy to move.

"You forgot this," Graham says, suddenly next to me. He's holding my purse.

I take it without saying a word. What is there to say? I can't go back. I can't undo what I've done. I can't make him like me again. I can't even blame him for hating me. At least one of us cares enough about Lily to look out for her.

The light changes and cars speed by. Not a single cab passes. I think about walking to Twenty-eighth Street or

Ninth Avenue or even Penn Station. But I don't move a muscle.

"I'm sorry," Graham says.

I shrug. It doesn't matter. Nothing matters.

Just as the light is turning red again, a livery driver stops. "Where to?"

Graham tells him Penn Station and asks how much. I don't hear the answer but it must be acceptable because he opens the car door. I climb in. We drive in silence.

"I don't know what happened back there," he says quietly. Maybe he doesn't want the driver to hear. "I was just dropping by on the way to a gig to tell you Lily was in bad shape. In case you're wondering, I told them I was Lily Carmichael to get in. Amazingly, it worked. Anyway, somehow or other I lost it completely. I was totally out of line. I'm sorry."

I shrug again as a tear slowly rolls down my cheek. The numbness is fading; pain is starting to return.

He doesn't say anything else until we're on the train. I pick a two-seater and he sits down next to me. "He called to tell her in the middle of her shift," Graham explains as we pull out of the station. The loudspeaker crackles but the announcements are unintelligible. "He wanted to share the good news as soon as possible."

I nod. That sounds just like the Jefferson Radley Carmichael the Third I know and despise. How did someone like him get to be a parent? Why isn't his sperm as useless as the rest of him? "The secretary?"

"No, the paralegal."

I'm surprised enough to face him. The blazing-sun-glare-of-death is gone from his face, and he looks as tired as I feel. "What?"

"He was cheating on the secretary with the paralegal. She's a twenty-five-year-old law student he met five months ago. The second their eyes met, he knew it was meant to be."

It's all bullshit. The fifty-something secretary and the twenty-something paralegal are just temporary names for a permanent problem called infidelity. No wonder Lily never dates a guy for more than ten minutes. She comes by her fears honestly.

I lean back in my seat and close my eyes, too tired to think about it. But I have to. "How's Vivienne taking it?"

"Not so good. She tried to trick Lily into signing an affidavit saying she wants her mom to have custody."

My eyes fly open. "What?"

"Told her it was a savings bond," he says with disgust. "Figured she wouldn't know the difference."

"Lily's not stupid."

"No, but her mother is. The orgy of mother-daughter bonding was to earn Lily's trust. I've gotta say," he adds, looking at me out of the corner of his eye, "living with someone that dumb can't be easy. I might choose the para-legal, too."

Graham is quiet for the rest of the ride. Exhausted, I press my head against the glass and try to get some of the lovely numbness back. It hurts too much to feel. It hurts too much to think of all the people I let down: Lily, Jessica, Graham, Lois, Mom, Dad, and somehow worst of all, myself. It's all so fucking stupid and so incredibly meaningless.

Tears begin falling again, this time in a thick stream. I'm actually crying, and no matter what I do, I can't make it stop. I have no control over anything. Maybe this is what a breakdown feels like. Maybe everything inside me cracked the moment Elton Valley pointed his smug, little malicious grin at me.

I keep my forehead pressed against the window, hoping Graham doesn't hear me sniffling. I don't want him to see I'm a total wreck. One look and he'd know it's not just this moment; it's my whole life. I've had enough humiliation for one day.

But then Graham puts a packet of tissues in my lap and I realize there isn't enough humiliation in the world for someone like me: who deserts her best friend, who lies to her mentor, who fools around with creeps, who lets the best opportunity of her life slip through her fingers because she's too busying partying to notice.

The tears are still falling when we arrive in Bellmore, but I'm too wiped out to care. I follow Graham down the escalator and climb into the cab he waves down. I move over to make room for him but he doesn't get in.

"You're not coming?" I ask, surprised. He seemed so determined to rush to Lily's side and hold her hand. The driver turns on the engine as I get out of the car.

"Nah. I'd only be in the way," he says.

I don't know what to make of this. Did he escort me to here just to make sure I didn't go back to the party? Does he really think that little of me? "You didn't have to come out here. I would've been fine on my own."

"No biggie. I was going home anyway."

I remember something he said earlier. "No you weren't. You had a gig."

Graham shrugs. "Gig, shmig. We have two a week. You looked like you needed company. It was the least I could do after . . ."

I nod. It's not necessary for him to say it again. No matter how sincerely he apologizes, it won't make me feel any better. "Well, I guess I'll, uh, see you around."

He presses his lips against my forehead so softly I almost don't feel it. But I do: the gentlest whisper that sets off rockets and fireworks and even a flare gun or two. I close my eyes. "Take care," he says softly.

The ridiculous tears well up again like I'm a fountain on someone's front lawn set to a timer (every half hour). Embarrassed, I lower my head and climb into the car. After a quick stop at a deli, we pull into Lily's driveway. The house is dark, except for a single bulb shining over the garage. I take out my phone and dial her number as the cab drives away.

"What's the star count?" Lily says when she answers the phone.

I look up. It's a totally cloudy night. "Zero."

"But it's still early, right? Plenty of time to make up for that," she says. "So, tell me, what's it like?"

I close my eyes and picture the scene. "Lot of beautiful people. Lots of Ultrasuede. Lots of martini glasses. Oh, and lots of purple neon. It was like being in one of those dance clubs at the beach."

"Sounds fabulous," she says with a sigh.

I shrug. "Yeah, but there was one big problem."

"What?"

"No cookie-dough ice cream."

"Huh?"

"Can you imagine?" I ask, walking to her door and ringing the bell. I can hear the *ding-dong* through the earpiece. "This fancy, exclusive New York City club that claims to cater to your every little whim didn't have a single scoop of cookie-dough ice cream on the premises. So I had to leave."

At that moment the door swings open and Lily is there, staring at me. Her eyes are as rimmed in red as mine and her face just as blotchy. What a fine pair we make.

Lily slowly lowers the phone to her side. "What about Scarlett?" she asks.

I step into the foyer and let the screen door slam behind me. "She didn't have any, either. Nor did her entourage, which, I promise you, was large enough to carry around a whole frozen-food section from the supermarket."

Lily laughs, a happy trickling sound that makes me think everything's going to be okay, but in a flash her face crumbles and she starts to cry. I drop the ice cream and wrap my arms around her.

"He's marrying her" is all she says.

"I know, honey, I know."

She sobs harder into my shoulder, her tears burning hot little trails along my skin. I tighten my arms and rub her back and wait for the storm to pass. I know there's nothing I can say to make it better, and because of that, I get—really, *really* get—for the first time why I have to be here. The only thing I can give her, aside from a soft touch and a soothing word, is the steadying calm of knowing somebody loves her.

I don't know how long we stand there like that, intertwined like ivy. Eventually the tears subside and Lily's breathing returns to normal. We both remember the ice cream at the exact same moment and laugh over the beige stain on the beige carpet. Lily grabs two spoons from the kitchen and insists we eat the melted cookie dough in the dining room, with its black Formica table that's used only for important guests.

We sit very close to each other in the large room, our giggles echoing off the stark white walls as she reenacts the affidavit scene with her mother. ("Of course it's a savings bond, darling, that's why it says, 'in God we trust.'" "Hey, Mom, I *can* read. That says, 'in Godbaum we trust.'") When she's done, she demands that I tell her every detail of the party from the moment I arrived. It seems so stupid and trivial in comparison, but she wants to think of something other than herself, which I totally understand. So I tell her the entire story, starting with the red carpet, continuing through the makeout session with Michael Davies, and ending with Jessica's sly introduction. I don't leave anything out, especially my own awful behavior. I want her to know the truth. The whole thing is still painful and horrible but already the sting is beginning to fade. Somehow Elton Valley's coldly superior, gotcha grin isn't as awful when you're impersonating it for your best friend.

I stay for hours. After we finish the soupy ice cream Lily digs through the kitchen cabinets and finds a box of expensive truffles her mother is saving for a Friends of the Library meeting. We eat every last one, defiantly leaving the box and the sticky Ben & Jerry's carton on the table as evidence. We dare her to call us on it.

By the time Lily grabs her keys at midnight to drive me home my belly hurts from laughing so hard. I can't remember the last time I felt so giddy.

It's drizzling slightly when we step outside, but Lily keeps the top down on her Miata and turns on the radio. "I Will Survive" blares from the speakers. It's tired and old and the most annoying song in the world, but I don't change the station. It's the right anthem for the right moment, so I turn the volume up high, and we both sing at the top of our lungs as the wind blows through our hair.

Lily was right. There was plenty of time to make up for a night without stars.

The *Savvy*
ADVANTAGE:
WHAT EVERY
SMART GIRL
SHOULD KNOW

When I get home, I confess everything to Mom. I start with Lily's stuff because it's real-life and important, but I eventually get to my own. I give it to her totally straight without any spin, which is hard. I want my mom's trust and respect, and I know with every word I say, I lose a little bit more of both.

Mom listens silently and doesn't interrupt, even when I get to the part where I drunkenly make out with a guy I don't like. I'm expecting total condemnation and a life sentence, but she's too tired to dole out disapproval or punishment. She simply kisses me on the cheek and says we'll talk about it tomorrow.

I get into bed at one-thirty, and even though I've never been so tired in my life, I can't fall asleep. My mind is racing from one thing to another, from reliving the worst moments of the day to imagining tomorrow to wondering about Graham's motives to kicking myself for blowing off the biggest opportunity of my life. Everything is in my head all at once.

After lying awake for an hour I switch on my lamp and reach for the collection of short stories I keep by my bedside for occasions like these. I open to "I'm the Only One" by Zadie Smith and start reading. The story is hard to get into because the first two pages are dense with text, and I flip ahead to see if it lightens up later. Toward the end it does, so I turn back to the first page, determined to concentrate.

But it's no use. My mind is still darting from Jessica to Graham to Lois, and all I can do is stare at the words without seeing them. Annoyed, I climb out of bed, sit down at the desk, boot up my laptop, and begin writing.

I'm still at my computer when Dad's alarm goes off at six-thirty. Mine chirps a half hour later just as I'm printing out a copy of my essay. Then I e-mail a version to myself, stretch, yawn, then jump into the shower. I'm so tired, I have to drink three cups of coffee at breakfast before I feel half alive, a development that troubles both my parents. Dad takes the third cup away from me before I can finish it.

"You're still growing," he says, not looking up from the newspaper.

On the train I read my essay in its entirety for the first time. I'm expecting it to be full of awkward phrases and badly expressed ideas but aside from a ton of typos, it's pretty okay. My first all-nighter and it actually paid off.

My satisfaction fades the second I step into the Mulhville-Moore building and is replaced by anxiety. The closer I get to the fortieth floor, the more butterflies flutter in my stomach. By the time the elevator doors open I'm ready to take the next train back to Bellmore.

I don't know what I think will happen, but there isn't a small group of editors with oak-tag signs saying CHRISSY GIBBONS SUCKS waiting for me in the *Savvy* lobby. Nobody shouts mean names as I walk to my desk. No one distributes an all-staff memo detailing my exploits or sends e-mails calling me a liar. As far as my colleagues at M-M Publishing are concerned, this is just another day at the office.

Keeping my head down, I make a few last changes to my Savvy Girl essay. Then I reread it one more time, print out the final version, and bring it to Lisa's office, hoping to hand it directly to the executive editor. I imagine her scanning the first few lines while I hover hesitantly by the door and then making some encouraging comment ("very nice," "strong start," "good use of adjectives") to give me a sense of what I've turned in. Because I don't have a clue. It's entirely possible that I've just made the biggest mistake of my life.

But Lisa's not there, so I leave it in her in-box and return to my desk feeling strangely deflated.

The day drags for two reasons. One: I'm thoroughly wiped out and can barely keep my eyes open. I'm even beyond the help of caffeine. When Michael Davies drops by my desk to let me down easy ("You're sweet and all, but I can't deal with all the drama. So we're good?"), I can only manage a pathetic half nod. Two: Every second of every minute of every hour, I expect to see Jessica. It's not a matter of if but when, and I just want to get the terrible moment over with. The waiting, the wondering, is killing me.

At four o'clock the editors call us into the conference room for an unscheduled all-staff meeting. The butterflies in my stomach, which never went away (although they did seem to settle in for a nap around lunchtime), start flapping their wings. Now that I'm about to see Jessica, I feel a cowardly desire to run and hide. Any bathroom stall would do.

So much for wanting to get the hard part over with.

There are only a handful of people in the room when I arrive, and although there are plenty of seats at the table, I sit on one of the long benches against the side wall. I want to be out of the way, in a dark corner where nobody can see me. Unfortunately, I'm hardly invisible and Hallie takes the cushion next to mine.

"What do you think this is about?" she asks as the room fills up. Still no Jessica.

Struggling to stifle a yawn, I tell her I have no idea.

"Beth thinks they're going to announce Savvy Girl."

Just the thought sets my heart racing. "Impossible. They said they would announce on the last day of the internship. That's next Friday. It's probably another endless meeting about the 401(k). I don't know why we have to go to these things. We don't have retirement plans or anything."

"Yeah. What was up with that accounting system they taught us last week? If I had an expense account, then, sure,

I'd love to know how to enter receipts. But I don't," she says, tapping her pen against her Filofax. The rhythmic sound is slowly lulling me to sleep. "It's publishing. Editors love to meet. Last summer I interned at *Glamour* and sometimes we met twice a week. It was crazy."

Hallie goes on to explain in minute detail the craziness of biweekly meetings, but I stop paying attention when she starts listing all the stories she wrote. Her need to brag is almost compulsive, and I can't stand to listen to it when I don't have anything to brag about in return.

Jessica walks into the room a few steps behind Lisa, and I stop pretending to listen to Hallie. Her eyes sweep the room as she looks for an empty chair, and I wait for the sizzle of awareness when our eyes meet, but she doesn't even notice me. I might as well not be there.

So this is what it's like to be in a fight with a tall, thin, beautiful, chic, ex-model, British fashion editor.

She takes a seat at the head of the table, near the slide projector, and immediately starts talking to Lois. Next to me Hallie continues her speech on brilliant articles she has written. Every so often I nod.

When we're all seated, Georgie starts the meeting. Her assistant doesn't pull down the screen, which means no PowerPoint presentation on sales figures or demo breakdowns. I cross my legs and lean forward, suddenly interested.

"Good afternoon. I apologize for this unscheduled interruption. I know you're all very busy, so I'll make this brief. As you know, today was the deadline for the Savvy Girl column."

Hallie stiffens. "I'm not ready for this," she whispers.

Neither am I. The butterflies in my stomach start flailing. It feels like they're trying to escape.

"As you know, we'd planned to announce the winner next Friday. But I read them this afternoon, and while they were all very good, I thought one was extra-special and I couldn't wait to share it with you. It's exactly what we're looking for."

She puts on her reading glasses and takes an essay out of a folder. It's impossible to tell from this distance whose essay it is. She begins reading:

"I'm not a Savvy Girl. I'm too easily impressed by the trappings of success. I'm too quickly wowed by money, fame and glamour. I'm too ready to believe that something is good or better simply because it's beautiful. I'll abandon my best friend to go to a party with strangers. I'll lie to my parents to win their approval. I'll betray the confidence of a mentor to get my own way. Give me a yard and I'll take a mile. Trust me and I'll let you down.

Have I always been like this? No. I'm what you commonly call a good kid. I get decent grades and head up the school newspaper. I'm nice to teachers, polite to parents, and patient with old people. I don't smoke or do drugs; I don't drink much. I've never had sex. I follow the rules and color between the lines and call when I'm going to be late. This is who I am.

Or rather: This is who I was.

This summer I realized just how little my values mean to me and how quickly I'll subvert them to fit in. It's the same old story: bright lights, big city, fabulous parties. All I wanted was for people to like me and to think I was like them. It was easy enough to seem urbane, clever, and jaded, to appear bored by the many fascinating and thrilling things that went on around me. But affecting sophistication affected me. The very act of pretending to be someone else made me someone else. I didn't know this could happen. I didn't know I was at risk for a personality transplant.

But maybe that's the point of being seventeen: You don't know yet all the things you don't know.

This is why it's such a dangerous age. At seventeen, we believe we're wise and full-grown adults. We get chosen out of three thousand other applicants to be interns at a glossy women's magazine in New York City and we think we're ready to run with the bulls. But we only wind up getting trampled underfoot.

It's hard for me to admit that I'm not ready for the big leagues. It's hard for me to accept that I'm not mature enough to handle adult responsibility. It's hard for me to confess in front of all my peers and colleagues that I'm not the person they—or I—thought I was. It's all hard, hard, hard.

This is something we tend to gloss over at Savvy. We see ourselves as cheerleaders on the sidelines rooting you across the finish line, and sometimes we don't acknowledge how tough things really are. We say you can lose weight in three easy steps or get rock-hard abs in three short months. We say that fat-free sour cream is just as yummy as full-fat and that a two-hundred-calorie snack will tide you over nicely till dinner. Well, it's not true. Fat-free sour cream tastes like glue and two hundred calories will leave you starving by four-thirty. But so what? You have to do it anyway because dieting is hard. Staying in shape is hard. Getting firm abs is hard. Saying you're sorry is hard. Owning up to mistakes is hard. Loving your parents for who they are is hard. Being true to yourself is hard.

Life is hard.

I know nobody wants to hear this. I don't, either. I'd much rather bury my head and pretend to love fat-free sour cream. But I can't. I've been through too much this summer to shut my eyes willfully at a few unpleasant truths. The only way to grow is through knowledge. The only way to learn is through accepting your ignorance. None of this feels comfortable to me yet (will it ever?), but I'm ready to do both. I'm ready to face life head-on without flinching, even if it's hard.

Because when I grow up, I want to be a savvy woman who can run with the bulls."

Georgie pauses, removes her glasses, and looks up. "And that, ladies, was by our first Savvy Girl columnist, Chrissy Gibbons."

The room is silent as people look to their right and then left, trying to figure out which one of the interchangeable interns is Chrissy Gibbons. Even Georgie isn't sure. Then—amazingly—Adele starts to clap. Lois follows.

"Ohmigod," Hallie says, throwing her arms around me like we're the final two contestants on *Survivor*. I can't believe she's genuinely happy for me. Her essay was so much better. "That was fabulous."

Everyone is clapping now. Several women who haven't looked at me since the intern breakfast come over to congratulate me on a great job. Simone gives me a hug. Georgie shakes my hand and says nice work. "I'm looking forward to next month's installment, Chrissy."

Flustered, I manage a garbled thank-you. I've been so focused on turning out the one column, I completely forgot there are eleven more. Oh, god.

People slowly filter out of the room as Lois pats me on the back. "I knew you could do it," she says admiringly. "I might have been a little concerned when you didn't hand in a draft but I understand now. It's very personal stuff. Exactly the kind of self-reflection we love at *Savvy*."

"Yeah," agrees Adele, who is hovering behind Lois. "It's perfect for us."

I thank them both, but it's painful to accept their compliments. I feel like a total fraud. What I said is true: I'm not a Savvy Girl. I don't deserve this.

When the room is finally empty, I sit down on the cushion, rest my head against the wall, and close my eyes. I'm too tired to think or to feel, so I simply absorb the beautiful silence. This is the first peaceful moment I've had in twenty-four hours. If I weren't afraid of getting locked in by the cleaning staff, I'd lay my head down and go to sleep.

I hear the door swish open but I'm too comfortable to move. Someone probably forgot a notebook or sweater. I wait for the sound of her leaving and when it doesn't come, I open my eyes.

Jessica is sitting opposite me in a black leather chair, carefully studying me like I'm some sort of alien life form. Embarrassed, I turn away, already breaking my promise to face life head-on without flinching. I'm totally useless.

"It's hard," she says conversationally, pausing a moment for emphasis, "to remember you're only seventeen. Or to understand what that means. By the time I was your age, I'd already gone through several men, three drug habits, and one career. I didn't think about what all this would mean for you."

It almost sounds like she's apologizing, which is unbearable. I'm the one who screwed up. I'm the one who took advantage. I'm the one who lied. "I'm sorry," I say, tears careening down my cheeks. "I'm so, *so* sorry."

Jessica runs her hands over my hot forehead. Her fingers are cool. "I know. I know, sweetie."

"I'm awful. Terrible. Evil."

She laughs. "No, you're young. And because you are, I'm going to say to you what I hope someone would say to my sister if she found herself in a similar situation: You're grounded. No more parties, no more alcohol, and certainly no more glamorous fashion editors. Come back after you graduate college and we'll reevaluate. All right?"

I nod and brush away the tears. She's being kind but it does nothing to lessen my shame. It only makes it worse. "All right."

"Good," she says, pulling me to my feet and threading her arm through mine. We walk back to my desk in silence. I'm tempted to apologize again and again, but I know she doesn't need to hear it. She understands. Amazingly.

"Thank you," I say softly when we reach my cube.

"You're welcome," she says, her eyes steady as she looks into mine. Then she smiles. "Now go home and get some sleep, chica. You look awful."

I laugh because I know it's true, and watch her walk away with an almost worshipful feeling in my heart. More than ever I know it: I want to be just like her when I grow up.

My cell phone rings, breaking me out of my half-catatonic state. I answer.

"Stay calm," Lily orders when I pick up. "Nothing's happened. I'm just checking in to see how you're doing."

"Hey, I'm supposed to do that. How *are* you? Did Vivienne say anything about the mess on her table?"

"She kissed me on the cheek and said she always hated that shiny black slab. Dad picked it out. Then she scratched it a few times with a kitchen knife. Apparently very therapeutic. She apologized for the affidavit and went to bed."

"Huh."

"I know. So how's your day after?"

"You won't believe it," I say, and break the good news. She shrieks and cheers for a full minute.

"I'm so proud of you," she says.

"Don't be. I don't deserve it."

Lily pooh-poohs what she calls my false modesty and says she'll be proud if she wants to. "Oh, by the way, Graham made me promise to apologize to you again. He feels awful about what happened."

Images from last night flash through my head. Michael's killer smile. Graham's burning-sun eyes. "It's not necessary."

"He thinks it is. He says he kinda freaked out when he saw you kissing Michael. He didn't know you were seeing anyone," she explains.

The implication is crystal clear but completely baffling.

I can't imagine what she's saying or trying to say. "Lily, I thought you liked him."

She laughs. "I do. He's great."

"No," I explain, the suspense killing me. "I thought you *liked* liked him."

"Honey, that was weeks ago and for, like, a split second. He liked you from the moment you met."

"Really?" I ask. It doesn't make sense. Nobody has ever liked me that quickly, certainly not when Lily is around.

"Yeah, he talks about you all the time."

I frown, disappointed. *This* is her evidence? "Has he ever come out and said he likes me?"

"Well," she says, considering, "not in so many words. But it's so obvious."

I'm silent.

"You have to trust me on this, Chris. The boy's crazy about you." When I don't respond, she adds, "He had a performance today at Juilliard. He had to cut out of here early to make it."

"So?" I ask petulantly. I'm annoyed she never got him to say it in so many words. I can't risk myself on a strong hunch. I have to know for sure.

"So he should be finishing up right about now. You might be able to catch him at Penn Station."

Put myself out there with no assured response? I shake my head. "I can't."

"You can." She's quiet for a moment. "Put down the

phone, turn off your computer, grab your bag, and get out of there."

It's the hardest thing I've ever done—harder than sitting quietly while Georgie read my essay to the entire staff—but I put down the phone, turn off my computer, grab my bag, and get out of there. I run to the elevator and press the button incessantly as I wait for the car to come. Usually there's one every thirty seconds but now it takes hours. When it finally arrives, it's stuffed with people but I don't care. I make them all inhale so I can fit.

Outside, I dash across the street and into the subway, pulling my MetroCard out of my wallet so fast everything spills. Fuck. Shit. Crap. I can hear the train coming as I pick up my change.

I miss the number 2 train by five seconds and have to stand on the suffocating platform for almost five minutes until another arrives.

"About time," I mutter as I watch it stop. There are hundreds of us waiting and we all surge forward at the same time. I squeeze onto the train and listen as the conductor tells everyone to move into the center of the car to fit more people.

Come on, come on, I think as the doors open and close. Someone's briefcase is blocking the door. This always happens. Can't people hold their things close? For god's sake, this is New York City. You're supposed to keep a stranglehold on your possessions.

By the time we pull out of Times Square it's five after six. I don't know anything about the Great Neck train schedule. I don't even know what line it's on.

Penn Station is the usual rush-hour mob scene, with commuters running in every direction to catch their trains, and as I watch them, I realize how stupid my plan is. There's no way I'll find him here at this hour. I might as well be looking for a needle in a haystack.

But just as I'm about to buy a consolation doughnut (relieved but not relieved, if you know what I mean), I see him by the vending machine. He's inserting his credit card. Feeling giddy, excited, and scared to death, I watch him take his ticket, then follow him down to track 19. The train is just pulling in as we get there. My heart beating furiously, I wait for the doors to open. He's only a few feet away from me now. I could tap him on the shoulder if I wanted to (and if I didn't mind sticking my arm in the face of the woman next to me).

The train doors open and we all push inside. Graham goes to the right and chooses a two-seater. I turn to the right, but there are five people in front of me and I'm terrified that one of them is going to take the seat next to him. They all pass. Thank god.

My heart in my throat, I sit down. I don't say anything, just look, watch, wait. At first he doesn't notice me but then he catches my reflection in the window and turns. The delight on his face, the sincerely-happy-to-see-you expression, takes my breath away and calms me down in the same moment. Amazingly, Lily is right.

"Hey," I say so casually we might have been sitting in his parents' living room.

He smiles, eyes crinkling in the corners. "Hey."

I lean back against the cushion and dig out my train ticket. I have no idea if it's good on this line. Out of the corner of my eye I can see him watching me and wondering.

"So," he finally says, "what's going on?"

Trying very hard to keep a straight face, I say, "I'm making sure you get home. I've noticed you have a tendency to take the wrong train and I didn't want it to happen again."

He examines me carefully, staring deeply into my eyes as if he's looking for something. Then he smiles again. He has *such* a smile. Not killer, no, but still deadly. "So you're just looking out for me?"

"It's a public service," I explain, my heart pounding. "I'd do it for anyone."

He takes my hand. "Do me a favor."

I look down at our clasped fingers, my skin tingling from the contact. Then I slowly raise my head and find him staring at me with the sweetest expression I've ever seen on anybody's face. I don't how I missed it. It's right there for any idiot to see.

"Sure," I say softly.

"Don't do it for anyone," he says, lowering his head. "Do it for me."

Mesmerized by his eyes, I breathe "okay" seconds before his mouth touches mine. His lips are warm and gentle and perfect and I feel myself sliding into sweet oblivion as he pulls me closer. And just before I can't think of anything at all, I marvel again at my own stupidity.

No, I'm not a Savvy Girl, but I'm getting there.

ACKNOWLEDGMENTS

THANKS TO:
my father, my brothers, the Linwoods,
Chris and Roell

AND:
Susan Ramer and Julie Tibbott

ALSO:
Rachel Orr, who gave me a little push